*HIGHLY
ILLOGICAL
BEHAVIOR*

HIGHLY ILLOGICAL BEHAVIOR

JOHN COREY WHALEY

DIAL BOOKS

DIAL BOOKS
An imprint of Penguin Random House LLC
375 Hudson Street • New York, NY 10014

Copyright © 2016 by John Corey Whaley

Library of Congress Cataloging-in-Publication Data
Names: Whaley, John Corey, author.
Title: Highly illogical behavior / John Corey Whaley.
Description: New York : Dial Books, [2016] * Summary: Agoraphobic sixteen-year-old Solomon has not left his house in three years, but Lisa is determined to change that—and to write a scholarship-winning essay based on the results.
Identifiers: LCCN 2015025530 * ISBN 9780525428183 (hardcover)
Subjects: | CYAC: Agoraphobia—Fiction. * Panic attacks—Fiction. * Friendship—Fiction. * Gays—Fiction.
Classification: LCC PZ7.W5458 Hi 2016 * DDC [Fic]—dc23
LC record available at http://lccn.loc.gov/2015025530

Printed in the United States of America
1 3 5 7 9 10 8 6 4 2
Design by Jason Henry * Text set in Melior

FOR SCOTTY

PART ONE
SPRING

ONE

SOLOMON REED

Solomon never needed to leave the house anyway. He had food. He had water. He could see the mountains from his bedroom window, and his parents were so busy all the time that he pretty much got to be sole ruler of the house. Jason and Valerie Reed let it be this way because, eventually, giving in to their son's condition was the only way to make him better. So, by the time he turned sixteen, he hadn't left the house in three years, two months, and one day. He was pale and chronically barefoot and it worked. It was the only thing that ever had.

He did his schoolwork online—usually finishing it before his parents were home every evening, with bed head and pajamas on. If the phone rang, he'd let it go to voice mail. And, on the rare occasion that someone knocked on the door, he would look through the peephole until whoever it was—a Girl Scout, a politician, or maybe a neighbor—would give up and leave. Solomon lived in the only world that would have him. And even though it was quiet and mundane and sometimes lonely, it never got out of control.

He hadn't made the decision lightly, and it should be said that he at least tried to make it out there for as long as possible, for as long as anyone like him *could*. Then one day trying wasn't enough, so he stripped down to his boxers and sat in the fountain in front of his junior high school. And right there, with his classmates and teachers watching, with the morning sun blinding him, he slowly leaned back until his entire body was underwater.

That was the last time Solomon Reed went to Upland Junior High and, within a matter of days, he started refusing to go outside altogether. It was better that way.

"It's better this way," he said to his mom, who begged him each morning to try harder.

And really, it was. His panic attacks had been happening since he was eleven, but over the course of just two years, he'd gone from having one every few months, to once a month, to twice, and so on. By the time he hopped into the fountain like a lunatic, he was having mild to severe panic attacks up to three times daily.

It was hell.

After the fountain, he realized what he had to do. Take away the things that make you panic and you won't panic. And then he spent three years wondering why everyone found that so hard to understand. All he was doing was living instead of dying. Some people get cancer. Some people get crazy. Nobody tries to take the chemo away.

Solomon was born and will, in all likelihood, die in Upland, California. Upland is a suburb of Los Angeles, just about an hour east of downtown. It's in a part of the state they call the Inland Empire, which really floats Solomon's boat because it sounds like something from *Star Trek*, which is a television show he knows far too much about.

His parents, Jason and Valerie, *don't* know too much about *Star Trek,* despite their son's insistence that it's a brilliant exploration of humanity. It makes him happy, though, so they'll watch an episode with him every now and then. They even ask questions about the characters from time to time just so they can see that excited look he gets.

Valerie Reed is a dentist with her own practice in Upland, and Jason builds movie sets on a studio lot in Burbank. You'd think this would lead to some great stories from work, but Jason's the kind of guy who thinks Dermot Mulroney and Dylan McDermott are interchangeable, so most of his celebrity sightings can't be trusted.

A week after he turned sixteen, Solomon was growing impatient as his dad tried to tell him about an actor he'd seen on set earlier that day.

"You know . . . the guy with the mustache. From the show . . . the show with the theme song . . ."

"That's every show on TV, Dad."

"Oh, you know the guy. The gun guy!"

"The *gun* guy? What does that even mean?"

"The guy. He holds the gun in the opening thing. I know you know the guy."

"I don't know. *Hawaii Five-O?*"

"That's a movie, not an actor," his dad said.

"It's a television show. How can you work in Hollywood?"

"You get your schoolwork done today?" Solomon's mom asked as she walked into the living room.

"This morning. How was work?"

"I got a new patient today."

"Keep bringing in those big bucks!" his dad joked. Nobody laughed.

"She says she went to Upland Junior High. Lisa Praytor? Does that ring a bell?"

"Nope," Solomon replied.

"Nice girl. Beautiful molars. But she's going to need to get those wisdom teeth out in a year or two or she'll have to get braces all over again."

"Did you have braces?" Solomon asked.

"Headgear. It was awful."

"Oh, it all makes sense now. You want to put others through the torture of your childhood."

"Don't analyze me."

"Solomon, stop analyzing your mother," his dad said from behind a book, one of those creepy mystery novels he was always reading.

"Anyway, she's a nice girl. Pretty too. Only one cavity."

Solomon knew good and well what was going on. His mom was doing that thing she did where she thought talking about some pretty girl would suddenly cure her son and have him walking right out the front door and straight to high school. It was innocent enough, but he hoped she wasn't actually that desperate for him to change. Because, if she was, then wouldn't these little moments, built up over time, eventually collapse into a mess?

He'd heard their conversations about him a few times. When he was ten he learned that if he held a plastic cup against his bedroom wall, he could hear everything his parents were saying in their bedroom. The last time he listened was when his mom asked his dad if they were going to be "stuck with him forever." After she said it, he didn't hear anything for a while. Then he realized it was because she'd started crying as soon as the words left her mouth. Hours later, Solomon was still awake wondering how to answer his mother's question. He eventually decided on a hard yes.

TWO

LISA PRAYTOR

Sometimes life just hands you the lemonade, straight up in a chilled glass with a little slice of lemon on top. For Lisa Praytor, junior and straight-A student at Upland High, meeting Solomon Reed's mother was that glass of lemonade. And it was going to change her life.

You may have known a Lisa Praytor at some point. She was the girl sitting at the front of your classroom, raising her hand to answer every single question the teacher asked. She stayed after school to work on the yearbook and as soon as she got home, she dove headfirst into her homework.

She'd always been one to keep a packed schedule, choosing at age eleven to live by the words of her great-aunt Dolores, who said, "Not a day on your calendar should ever be empty. It's bad luck. Twenty-four hours of wasted opportunity."

Not even an offer from her boyfriend to drive to the coast and watch the sunset could tempt her off schedule. And Clark Robbins was the kind of guy who asked her to do things like that all the time. He was handsome without being threatening, and his tree-bark brown hair parted in a way that was particularly appealing to Lisa. On the day that Lisa met Solomon's mom, she'd been dating Clark for a year and seventeen days. She had it marked on her calendar for proof.

During eighth grade, after a seventh grader had an episode in front of the school, Lisa wrote an op-ed piece for the Upland Junior High *Register* to defend the boy—a scathing essay on the importance of empathy. It didn't go over well with her classmates and until the end of the year, rumors swirled around that Lisa was secretly dating the crazy kid who jumped into the fountain.

Had it not been for the student body of nearly one thousand at Upland Junior High, Lisa may not have been able to escape her failed attempt at heroism when she got to high school. She did, though, and most of her friends and classmates eventually forgot about it altogether.

But not Lisa. She'd seen him that day—this skinny little guy with messy hair taking his shirt off and dropping his pants and walking that slow, quiet walk toward the water. She never knew him, really, but she'd always thought he looked nice, like the kind of guy who'd hold a door open for someone else without a thought. And she'd always hoped that someday she'd see him again or, at the very least, hear that he was doing okay.

Then one day, Lisa saw an advertisement for Valerie Reed's dental practice in the local newspaper. It took one Internet search to confirm that this was Solomon's mother. She'd never really been looking for the fountain kid, despite thinking about him from time to time and wondering where he'd ended up. But the second she realized she'd found him, she knew she had to get to him as soon as possible. And the only way to do that was to make an appointment with his mom. At the very least, Lisa would get a nice teeth cleaning and a free toothbrush. At the very best, she'd make all her dreams come true.

"So, where do you go to school?" Dr. Valerie Reed asked as she sat down to examine Lisa's teeth. It was March twenty-fourth, a Tuesday, and Lisa was having a really hard time not asking a million questions about Solomon.

"Upland High. Are you Solomon's mother?"

"Yes," she answered, slightly taken aback.

"I went to junior high with him. His picture's on the wall," she smiled, pointing across the room to a photograph of Valerie, Jason, and Solomon hanging by the window.

"You knew him?" Valerie asked.

"*Knew* him?" Lisa asked. "Oh! Did he . . . ?"

"No. God no. Sorry," Valerie said. "He just doesn't get out much."

"Private school? Western Christian?"

"He's homeschooled."

"You do that *and* this?" Lisa asked.

"It's all online. Okay, lean back for me. Open wide."

"I was there you know," Lisa said, sitting straight up.

"Where?" Dr. Reed asked. She was beginning to look a little frustrated.

"That morning. I saw your son . . . I saw his *incident*."

"It was a panic attack," she said. "Can I get a look at those teeth now?"

"Just one more thing," Lisa said.

"Go on."

"Why doesn't he get out much?"

Dr. Reed stared down at her in silence, her mouth covered with a blue paper mask, but her eyes searching for the right answer. And just when she went to speak, Lisa interrupted her.

"It's just . . . no one's seen him in so long. He was there and then he wasn't. It's strange is all. I thought maybe he went off to boarding school or something."

"He made it one day at Western Christian. What do you do if your kid won't leave the house?"

"Homeschool him?"

"It was our only option. Open wide."

As soon as Dr. Reed was done, Lisa picked right back up where she'd left off, not even waiting for her chair to be all the way upright again.

"When was the last time he left the house?"

"You sure are inquisitive, aren't you?"

"I'm sorry. Gosh, I'm so sorry. I never meant to be nosy. I've just thought a lot about him over the last few years and when I realized you were his mom, I guess I got too excited."

"It's okay," she said. "I'm just glad somebody remembers him. It's been three years. A little over, actually."

"Is he okay?"

"Mostly, yeah. We make it work."

"Must get lonely," Lisa said.

"You'd think that, yes."

"Does he have any friends?"

"Not anymore. Used to though. You guys all grow up so fast. He just couldn't keep up."

"Can you tell him I say hello? I doubt he'll know who I am, but just, you know, if it's not weird."

"I'll tell him, Lisa. And I'll see you next Tuesday to get this cavity fixed up."

Lying to adults was a little easier for Lisa than lying to her peers. Just like herself, none of her friends or classmates really trusted anyone, so lying was hard to get away with. But take someone like Valerie Reed, DDS, probably born in the late seventies to Southern California liberals, and you've got an easy target—someone who wants to trust everyone so much that they don't see a lie when it's slapping them right in the face.

In the grand scheme of things, Lisa knew it was harmless, a necessary step in taking her master plan from concept to actuality. And what a plan it was.

She was going to fix Solomon Reed.

Her life depended on it.

THREE
SOLOMON REED

Therapy didn't really work on Solomon because he didn't want it to. They tried taking him to someone when he was twelve, after realizing his tantrums and crying fits were more than just being a spoiled suburban kid. But he wouldn't talk to the therapist. Not a single word. And what were Jason and Valerie supposed to do? How do you discipline someone who *wants* to spend all day in his room? If they grounded him from the computer or TV, he'd just read books all day. And neither of them was going to start taking his books away.

He'd been a quiet, shy kid at school. The kid slumping in his desk in the back of the room that still managed to get A's and B's. There, he'd perfected the art of invisibility. But, at home, he laughed and joked around with his parents. He even listened to music too loud sometimes and sang made-up songs while he helped do dishes or set the table.

He was still in therapy when he had his meltdown at school, and so Jason and Valerie decided to try a new therapist—one who charged twice as much. Solomon went and, like always, said nothing. But he listened. He listened very well and as soon as his first session was over, he'd figured out a way to quit seeing *this* therapist, too. And he wouldn't even have to lie about it.

"She thinks you guys are abusing me or something."

"She said that?" his dad asked.

"Didn't have to," he answered. "Asked me all about your work schedules and whether or not you guys fight or yell. She's out for blood. I'm not going back."

And he didn't. Who were they to argue against it, either? When he was home, he was better. He was calm and happy and easy to get along with. The panic attacks were few and far between, and even though they'd never admit it, it actually made their lives much easier. No parent-teacher conferences, no driving him to school in the mornings and picking him up in the afternoons. At just thirteen years old, he needed very little from his parents and even less from the world. He wasn't bored or lonely or sad. He was safe. He could breathe. He could relax.

Solomon never had a lot of friends in school, just kids he'd say hi to or trade homework answers with from time to time. But, somehow he'd always end up having lunch with this kid named Grant Larsen. Grant was that sort to constantly talk about *hot girls* and action movies and which teachers he hated most. That is, when he wasn't bragging about his dad's "cool job" for an electric car company.

"Then why don't you guys have one?" Solomon would ask him.

"We don't have any way to charge it at home yet. But, soon, man. Real soon."

Grant didn't mind so much that Solomon never talked about girls or bragged about *his* dad's cool job. He just liked being listened to and that happened to be one of Solomon's strong suits. He'd nod and respond with one or two word answers. It was the only way he could sit there surrounded by hundreds of loud kids without freaking out. He would focus on Grant and keep quiet. Any more attention than that, and he risked having a panic attack right there in front of everyone. Like the one that eventually sealed his fate as the crazy kid.

To his credit, Grant *did* come to see Solomon after the fountain. But, at home, Solomon wasn't the muted listener he'd been at school. He was himself. And that was someone who Grant didn't seem to like very much.

"You want to play a game or something?" Solomon asked one day, just a few weeks after leaving school.

"What kind? You got a PlayStation?"

"Oh. No. I suck at video games. I meant a card game or something. You like strategy games?"

"Are you asking me to play Dungeons and Dragons? Because hell no. I'd like to not die a virgin."

"That doesn't even make sense."

"Tell that to my uncle Eric. Plays those nerdy games with all his nerdy friends all the time and my mom says he'll probably be alone forever."

"She sounds nice," Solomon said under his breath.

"Don't be a dick, I'm just trying to say it's a little lame."

It wasn't lame. Not even a little. And it didn't take long for Solomon to realize that he didn't need a friend. Which worked out well, because after a few months and a few more failed attempts at hanging out, Grant eventually stopped coming over altogether. His parents asked him a few times what Grant was up to, why he'd been so busy, and Solomon just shrugged it off and said he didn't know. He knew. He was busy boring someone new to death.

See, Solomon's world wasn't lonely like you'd think. It wasn't dark and sad. It was small, sure, but it was comfortable. Why would it need to be anything but that? He knew his parents worried, though, and that was really the only thing that bothered him. What he wished, more than anything, was to be able to explain to them how much better it was now. But judging from their silence on the issue, and his lack of a therapist, he figured they already knew.

FOUR
LISA PRAYTOR

Lisa had learned some important things from her mother. Like how to put on mascara while driving and what time of year it's okay to wear white shoes. But, mostly, Lisa learned that if she settled for a life she didn't want, then she'd end up just like her—overworked, mildly depressed, and failing miserably at a third marriage.

Lisa wanted more than Upland, California. It wasn't the worst place on earth, by any means, but it wasn't *her* place. Someone like Clark could live there forever, happy enough to have a quiet little life and never make too many waves. But Lisa needed something bigger. She wanted to be important. And that wasn't going to happen in the Inland Empire. Luckily, with her junior year coming to a close, Lisa saw an end in sight. And now that she had an appointment to see Solomon Reed's mom again, she was feeling pretty confident about her escape plan.

She still wasn't sure what to do about Clark, though. She loved him. It was hard not to, but every attempt she'd made at taking things to the next level had been shot down.

He didn't want to talk about college, always saying he just wasn't ready yet. And, despite his looks and confidence, it turned out he wasn't ready for some other things, either.

Clark wanted to wait. Lisa wasn't sure what, exactly, he wanted to wait for, but every time she tried to initiate anything even close to sex, he'd remind her that it wasn't the right time yet.

Of course she never once considered that the problem could be her.

"He's religious," she told her friend Janis on the phone. "That's why, right?"

Janis Plutko had been Lisa's best friend since the first grade. But, ever since she'd become a born-again Christian sophomore year, Lisa had felt a lot of distance from her. She didn't have a problem with it, but sometimes she wasn't so sure Janis knew the difference between being religious and acting that way.

"*Please*," Janis said. "I've dated three guys from Sunday School and every single one tried to feel me up. God's not your problem, Lisa."

"Well, what is it then? And don't say it's me. It's not."

"Lisa . . . he's on the water polo team *and* he has three older brothers," Janis said.

"What? Not again, Janis. He's *not* gay."

"Scientifically and superficially, these facts do not help his case for heterosexuality."

"What the hell are you talking about?"

"They say the more older brothers you have, the more likely you are to be homosexual. For males, at least. And do I even have to explain to you why water polo is gay?"

"Boys in Speedos playing around in a pool," Lisa said. "I get it. But he's not gay."

"Whatever you want to tell yourself, Lisa. But don't count this out. I have an instinct for these things. Best gaydar in town."

"The thing is, I don't really care that much right now."

"Lisa . . . I think you should probably care about something like this."

"Maybe everyone else should just care less about it. I've got too much to do anyway. Sex should be the last thing on my mind."

"See, you'd make a great Christian. Maybe just start going to church and he'll be all over you."

"I'm afraid I'd catch on fire as soon as I walked in."

"I'd be afraid of that too," Janis snapped.

"I love him. I'm pretty sure he loves me. So, for now, what's it matter?"

"This conversation started because of *your* sexual frustration."

"Even so. Like I said: sex is distracting. I need to focus on school and on getting out of here."

"Will you tell me about the dentist now?" Janis asked.

"She was nice. And I was right. He hasn't left the house in *years*."

"Fascinating," Janis said. "I wouldn't leave the house either if I'd done what he did."

"He couldn't help it," Lisa defended.

"Honestly, I don't know why you care so much about a kid you never met."

Lisa's plan had been taking shape for some time before

she actually met Solomon's mother, but she wasn't quite ready to tell Janis about it. Sometimes when you're doing something you maybe shouldn't be doing in the first place, the last thing you need is someone like Janis to tell you why you shouldn't be doing it. Lisa was smart enough to know the risks, and she'd already made up her mind.

Later that evening, at Clark's house, Lisa tried bringing up college to see if she could get some idea of what was going on in that head of his.

"Given any more thought to schools on the East Coast?" she asked.

"I was researching the other day," Clark replied. "Then I felt way too grown up and played video games instead."

"Well, I finally decided for sure. So, maybe you can plan around where I go."

"Okay. Where?"

"Woodlawn University. They have the second highest ranked psychology program in the country."

"Why not go for the first?"

"Because I *know* I can be top of my class at one and I'm slightly unsure I could be at the other."

"You're like Lady Macbeth without the murder."

"Thank you. You have no idea how much of a compliment that is to me."

"So, I should be looking at schools close by? Where is that, Oregon?"

"Maryland," she corrected. "Baltimore."

"I always wanted to see Poe's grave."

"Ridiculous," she said. "I have never understood this

universal fascination with gravesites. It's morbid and just . . . sad."

"I go to my granddad's grave sometimes. It's nice."

"Sorry."

"Doesn't matter to me," he said. "I like what I like, you like what you like."

"What do you do there? Just look at it and be sad?"

"No. Usually I just pray or talk to my granddad like he's still here. It honestly makes me happier than it does sad."

"People are strange, aren't they?"

"Is that why you're so dead set on fixing us all?" Clark asked.

"Not you," she said quickly. "You're good like you are."

"Thanks. So . . . Woodlaw . . ."

"*Woodlawn*," she corrected.

"Yeah, that. Can you get in?"

"With my eyes closed."

"What do you have to do? An essay or something?"

"Yeah. *My personal experience with mental illness.*"

"Shouldn't be too hard," he laughed. "You can just write about your mom. Or maybe *my* mom. She's legitimately insane."

"No. It has to be unique. It has to be the best one they read. Maybe the best one they've *ever* read. They give one scholarship a year. Full ride."

And she knew exactly what she was going to write about. It had practically hit her over the head the second she saw Dr. Reed's ad in the paper. She needed to find Solomon, charm him, and counsel him back to health. Then, she'd record it all in her essay to Woodlawn and be well on her way to securing her place among the greatest psychological minds of the twenty-first century. They'd be naming a building after her by the time she had grandkids.

But, she'd need to get started soon if she wanted to have guaranteed success. Especially since, by the sound of it, she could be dealing with a full-blown agoraphobe. That isn't something a person can conquer in a few weeks. Lisa would need several months with him to make the kind of progress she wanted—and she was already nearing the end of her junior year. That would allow just enough time to get her application in early. She wouldn't settle for being wait-listed and she wasn't about to apply to the third best psych program in the country. This was where she belonged and it was where she'd end up, no matter what.

"I'm going to write about my cousin," Lisa said.

"The one in the *place*?"

"Institution," she corrected. "I met him once. He gets out sometimes. Gets to come home for a weekend or two a year. It's weird. I've always wanted to talk to him or try to get to know him. I never do though."

"I'd be careful there," Clark advised. "No telling what could be wrong if he has to live away from everyone like that."

"No telling," she said. "But maybe I'll try to talk to him anyway."

Despite her interest in psychology, Lisa wasn't really planning to talk to her cousin, or anyone in her family for that matter. She could barely stand being in a room with her mom and her dad's birthday cards quit coming when she turned nine. She just needed a good cover so Clark wouldn't find out about Solomon. Not yet, anyway. You don't go telling your boyfriend that you need to spend a few months with another guy, especially one with a history of emotional instability and public meltdowns. She'd find the right time. Ignorance was bliss to Clark, so she was just doing him a favor anyway. He could wait a little longer to find out about her project. After all, it seemed like he really liked waiting on things.

FIVE

SOLOMON REED

By most people's standards, Solomon was a pretty weird kid. There was the agoraphobic thing, sure, but there were other things, too. He had impossibly weird eating habits, refusing to eat anything green, without exception, and having a substantial fear of coconut. Most days, he walked around half-clothed with a persistent case of bed head and a red line across his stomach where he'd rested the edge of his laptop while he did his schoolwork or streamed movies online. And, despite being terrible at video games, he'd ask his dad to play them just so he could watch, for hours and hours.

Oh, and he said his thoughts aloud sometimes. Not all the time, but often enough so his parents expected to round a corner and hear him saying something that made no sense to anyone else. The day after his mom met Lisa Praytor, she walked into his room at just the right time.

"Antwerp," he said, sitting at his desk and not realizing she was behind him.

"Who're you calling a twerp, twerp?" she said.

He spun around slowly in his chair until he was facing

her. His cheeks were a little red, but they'd be back to normal soon enough. He spent a *lot* of time with his parents, so there were few things left that could embarrass him.

"You know that new patient I was telling you about? The one from your school?"

"Lisa something?"

"Praytor," she said. "She sure was asking a lot about you."

"Well, it seems like she's all you can talk about lately. Are you trying to say I don't have perfect molars? Are you going to trade me in?"

"I haven't ruled it out."

"And she was asking a lot about me? That's creepy, Mom."

"She wasn't creepy at all. A little nosy, I guess. But not creepy. It's nice to know someone out there's thinking about you, isn't it?"

Solomon didn't really know what to say. So someone out there had been thinking about him. Great. What was he supposed to do with that—invite her over for brunch?

"I guess."

"It wouldn't hurt you to have a friend or two, you know?"

"We're not friends? You're saying we're not friends?" he joked, raising his voice and using a mobster accent.

"I'm saying your only friends shouldn't be middle aged and they certainly shouldn't be your parents."

"I don't see anything wrong with it," he said.

"Oh my God." She grabbed both sides of his face. "You're as hopeless as your dad."

Valerie Reed lived with older and younger versions of the same man—a minimalist introvert who never talked about his feelings and obsessed over ridiculous things. She managed to make it through their weekly viewings of old science fiction films and the in-depth conversations that would always follow. But she *did* like to joke that watching movies with them was "like pulling teeth." Get it? Of course you do.

"You know, you could probably reconnect with some of your old school friends online," she continued.

"Why would I want to do that, Mom?"

"For fun. I don't know."

"I have plenty of fun," he said.

"Fine," she raised one hand into the air and walked away. "I've got to go pay bills."

Solomon wondered if he'd ever have his own bills to pay. He didn't plan on leaving the house again. Ever. But even at sixteen he was starting to feel guilty for always being there—and for planning to always be there. His parents weren't the type to sit around growing old. He knew they'd want to travel or maybe even move somewhere else after retirement. On some days, especially when his mom would hint at him getting better in even a small way, he felt like the biggest and only problem in their lives. And he didn't want *his* cure to be their life sentence.

After his mom left the room, Solomon went back to his schoolwork. But, every now and then, he'd get online and do research. He didn't miss much about the outside world— Target sometimes, with its organized shelves and relaxing department store music. Some of his favorite restaurants, sure. Oh, and he really missed the way it smelled outside when it was about to rain, and the way the heavy drops would feel on his skin. This, though, he'd been able to enjoy by sticking his arm out of a window from time to time. Water calmed him down. He didn't know why, but it helped. He'd lie in the bath for an hour or more, his eyes closed, focusing his attention on the whirring of the bathroom vent. And that blocked it all out, anything that could make him worse, any thoughts that could start looping around and around in his mind. He knew that when it happened, he was supposed to close his eyes and count to ten and take slow, deep breaths. But that never worked like the water did.

So, for weeks, he'd been secretly working up the nerve to ask his parents for a pool. But how could he even mention the idea of it if he couldn't promise to go outside? He thought maybe he'd be ready by the time they could have a pool put in since he wasn't especially afraid of the outdoors anyway. It was the potential chaos that lay beyond their yard that scared him. Plus, he could damn sure use the exercise, because running on a treadmill had become mind-numbing. It's just that when you're afraid of dying, you'll do whatever it takes to keep yourself pretty healthy and the pool would help. He'd been fantasizing for weeks about waking up every morning and starting the day with a long swim. And, as much as he hated to admit it even to himself, he would imagine the warm beams of sun heating up his skin and eventually helping him look less like a walking corpse. Even in his isolation, Solomon wasn't completely immune to superficiality. He didn't know why he cared about his looks, but he did. And, at the very least, he hoped it was one more sign to his parents that his life was sustainable and not some statement against civilization.

Solomon hoped maybe if they thought it would help him, his parents would say yes to the pool. But, sitting there at his computer, thinking about what he'd be expected to do, his breathing starts to pick up. He didn't want to waste their money, sure, but most of all, he didn't want to give them hope and then let them down. He turned away from the computer, and bent forward, resting his elbows on his knees and hanging his head down as low as he could.

This is how it always started. Everything would be fine and then a sudden sinking feeling would come over him, like his chest was going to cave in. He could feel his heart bumping up against his rib cage, wanting out, quickening with every beat and then radiating down his arms and up to his temples. It vibrated him, making everything he saw bounce around like the world was just photographs being flipped in front of him. And with everything around him muffled, but still noisy, all he could do was focus on breathing and close his eyes tight and count.

Every number had an image attached to it. He saw himself standing at the back door, looking out at a brand-new pool, his parents beside him. And then he saw the looks of disappointment on their faces when they realized he was frozen in place and that it had all been for nothing.

When he got to one hundred, he sat back up and closed his laptop. He needed a break. He couldn't think about the pool anymore. He couldn't think about what the pool meant, to him or to them. He couldn't do anything but go to the garage, lie on the cold cement floor, and close his eyes again. The panic attacks drained him, like he'd just run a marathon, so it always took a little while to recover. So he lay there in the dark without them ever knowing he wasn't okay. Because he'd learned a long time ago that the better they thought he was, the longer he could live this way.

SIX

LISA PRAYTOR

One week after her first appointment, Lisa was back in Dr. Reed's office and waiting to get her cavity filled. She'd written a letter, which was sealed in a light blue envelope and tucked into the front pocket of her hoodie. She'd start with that, and if it didn't get her closer to Solomon, she'd find another way. She was almost certain she could convince Dr. Reed that her son needed a friend, but she was hoping the letter would get her in sooner.

It had been a long day at school, with three tests and a Student Council meeting, but Lisa still managed to exude a level of energy that no one in the small dental office could match. This wasn't her usual demeanor. She was more of a pragmatic know-it-all with control issues, but she was smart enough to know that you catch more flies with honey, so this cheery, inquisitive version of herself seemed like the best way to charm Dr. Reed.

Once seated in the exam chair, she chitchatted with the dental hygienist, Cathy, who was setting out some tools. But her eyes kept wandering over to the family photo hanging on the wall by the window—the photograph of

Solomon Reed the way he was when she last saw him, only not soaking wet and hyperventilating. She wondered what he looked like now, having witnessed firsthand what three years in the life of a teenage boy can do. Three years before, Clark had been a chubby eighth grader with acne problems and now look at him.

"Well, Lisa, you ready to get that cavity filled?" Dr. Reed asked, walking in and taking a seat next to the exam chair.

"You know it," Lisa answered. "How's life?"

"Life's good. Same as last week. Very busy."

She didn't give Lisa much opportunity to speak after that, quickly asking her to open wide and getting started on the anesthetic. Valerie Reed was a beautiful woman. She had laugh lines around her eyes and mouth, but the kind that make you envious of whatever put them there. Lisa had expected a hardened, maybe bitter person to be this troubled boy's mother, but Valerie Reed seemed as happy as could be.

"What's he like?" Lisa asked, her face half numb.

"Who? Solomon? Gosh. He's just *Solomon.*"

"Oh. Well, what does he like to do?"

"He likes to watch TV and read books. He's just like his dad."

"So how come that's the most recent picture I see around here?" she said.

"I don't know, Lisa. We don't take too many pictures just sitting around the house. And I think maybe I lucked out with the one teenager on earth who doesn't constantly take selfies."

"It's about insecurity," Lisa said. "I don't get it, either.

Maybe Solomon and I are just mature for our ages?"

"He has his moments."

"Can you give this to him?" Lisa pulled out the letter. "I know maybe it's weird. But, I just thought he might like it. You can even read it first if you want."

Dr. Reed looked down at the envelope and smirked a little, like she wasn't surprised at all that Lisa had written it.

"No, no. I don't need to do that. I'll give it to him. I can't promise you'll ever hear back, but I can promise he'll get it."

"Thank you so much."

As Dr. Reed filled the cavity in her lower right second bicuspid, Lisa closed her eyes and let her mind wander with the sound of the drill drowning out all the noise of the dental office. She thought about lonely Solomon Reed, sitting in a house all by himself with no clue that she was about to change his life. And even though there were a couple of fingers and a suction tube in her mouth, Lisa managed a smile.

When she got home, Clark was waiting in her driveway with a milk shake in his hand. He did things like that all the time, and it still surprised her.

"I can't feel half my face," she said, once out of her car.

"Can you feel this?" He stepped forward and poked her cheek.

"Nope."

"Weird. I've never had a cavity, so, you know, I wouldn't really know."

"Yeah, yeah. Gimme my milk shake."

"Oh, this milk shake? No, this is *my* milk shake."

He took a sip and then held it high above his head

where she couldn't reach. He was tall anyway, about 6'1",
and with his long, apish arms in the air, Lisa was screwed.
So she went for his biggest weakness and started for his
underarms. Being tickled made him physically ill, something left over from having grown up with all those older
brothers. He practically threw the milk shake at her to
make her stop.

"Mean," he said. "You're just stone-cold mean."

"Can we go inside now? I think the lidocaine's making
me woozy."

In her room, Lisa finished her homework while Clark
flipped through a magazine and kept her company. He had
homework, too, but he was more the kind of guy to say
he'd wake up early the next morning and do it and then
botch the whole plan and get the answers from one of his
classmates instead. He was smart, but not as smart as he
was handsome. And not near as smart as he was athletic.
Water polo was his life, mostly, but the season was over
now so he spent most of his free time with Lisa—so much
of it that she was starting to wonder where the hell all of
his friends were.

"Where the hell are all of your friends?" she asked,
slurring a little.

"The guys from the team? I don't know. Probably with
their girlfriends."

"It just seems like you haven't hung out with them lately."

"I'm sure I haven't missed much," he said. "They pretty
much drink beer and talk about sex. It's exactly what you'd
imagine."

So, Clark was bored with his friends. That would make

a lot of sense, seeing as most of them were fairly boring. Lisa was more of a one-close-friend type of person and had always had trouble fitting in with Clark's teammates and their girlfriends. But this was her first time realizing that maybe Clark felt the same way.

"How's the college essay?" he asked.

"Slow," she said.

"Are you still going to write about your cousin?"

Lisa needed to tell him about Solomon. She knew she could keep lying, but she'd already cleared her spring and summer to spend time helping Solomon get better, to make sure she'd actually have something to write about, something groundbreaking enough to get her that scholarship. Plus, Clark trusted Lisa and even if he *did* think her plan was unethical, he'd never try to talk her out of it. Or, at least, he'd never succeed at it.

"Hey, do you remember me telling you about that kid who jumped in the fountain in eighth grade?" she asked.

"I do," he answered. "What about him?"

"I found him."

"I didn't know you were looking for him."

"I wasn't. It's the weirdest thing. My new dentist is his mom. I didn't piece it together until I saw a picture of him in her office. Crazy, right?"

"Totally. Where's he been?"

"Home."

"Oh. That's kind of boring. I was hoping for something more dramatic."

"He's *only* been home," she says. "Nowhere else."

"Since eighth grade?"

"Yep."

"Weird. What do you think's wrong with him?"

"Well, lots of things, probably. You don't become home-bound for no reason. His mom said he had panic attacks, like at the fountain, so I'm guessing they kept getting worse and worse. So, preliminarily, I'd say he's got severe anxi-ety disorder that's contributed to a very persistent case of agoraphobia. And I wouldn't be surprised if he's got some obsessive compulsive tendencies as well."

"That's sad."

"I'm going to ask you something and I want you to promise to be completely honest with me. Okay?"

"Okay. . . ."

"I want to meet Solomon Reed. I don't know why I need to do it, but I do. And I think maybe I can make that hap-pen."

"Okay." He laughed. "This is . . . unexpected."

"It's just . . . you know . . . I've thought about him so much and wondered if he was okay and maybe it sounds crazy, but I just need to see for myself."

"Lisa, you didn't even know the guy."

"I know. But what if I can help him, Clark? This is what I want to do with my life and I feel like passing up an opportunity like this is . . ."

"I'm not stupid," he interrupted. "This is for the essay, right?"

She didn't say anything, but she nodded her head with her eyes lowered, afraid to see the disapproval on his face.

"How long have you been planning this?" he asked.

"Weeks," she confessed. "I'm sorry. I didn't want to

make it a big deal if it wasn't going to come to anything. But his mom's giving him a letter I wrote. Hopefully he'll respond."

"A letter? You wrote him a letter? Who are you, Lisa? My God."

"It's important to me, Clark. I can help him."

"You never wrote me a letter."

"Oh come on. You're jealous? Lock yourself away inside a house for three years and I'll write one up."

"That's not funny," he said.

"It's a little funny. I know it sounds awful, but I can help him. I need him and he needs me. It's not just about the scholarship. But, say the word and I'll stop."

He wasn't going to stop Lisa from doing anything and she knew it. And she could hardly expect him to be jealous over Solomon, especially after she'd been so up front about it. She knew it *was* weird that she'd reached out to him the way she had. But she also knew that there were a lot of people in the world who regretted never doing the things they felt were right because they were afraid of seeming strange or crazy. Lisa wouldn't settle for that sort of mediocre existence, one bound by invisible social cues. And she had a good feeling that someone like Solomon Reed would appreciate that.

SEVEN
SOLOMON REED

Solomon had never gotten a letter before. Ever. It was 2015, after all, and even if he *had* been more social, or perhaps not been a shut-in for almost a fifth of his life, he still could've probably gone on forever without getting one. So, when his mom handed him the blue envelope with his name scribbled on the front, he looked at her like she'd just handed him a rotary telephone or something.

"What do I do with this?" he asked.

"Read it, dummy," she said, rolling her eyes as she walked away.

Solomon ripped it open at one end, slid the letter out, and unfolded it, looking around the kitchen like maybe he was being pranked or something.

It read:

Dear Solomon,
You don't know me and I doubt you've ever even
heard of me, but my name is Lisa Praytor and
I want to be your friend. I know that sounds
ridiculous. Of course it does! But I also know that

*you can't go through life never pursuing what it is
you really want, and, for whatever reason, at this
time in my life, right now, I want to be your friend. I
saw you that last day you went to school. I saw you
and I was so scared for you. And, if you're still even
reading this, I want you to know that I've spent
years trying to figure out just why that boy jumped
into the fountain that morning at Upland Junior
High. Then, by some act of God herself, my new
dentist turns out to be your MOTHER. This universe
sends us signs sometimes and whatever you believe
or don't believe, this means something. I know your
situation is different from mine; I know you have
chosen to live a certain way and I respect that. So,
I hope you'll at least give some thought into having
a friend out here. I could sure use one and I bet, at
the very least, you could use a little conversation
from someone who doesn't know what the word
"escrow" means.
Sincerely,
Lisa Praytor
909-555-8010*

"I don't need a friend," he said aloud to himself.

"Are you hearing voices, Sol?" his mom teased from the other room.

Solomon walked out with the letter in his hand and stared right at her. She shook her head a little, and he could tell she was trying to keep her smile as best she could.

"It'll turn out just like Grant," he said. "Why bother?"

"Honey, Grant was a jerk."

"He was just normal," Solomon defended. "I don't know how to be around people like that."

"Are you saying I'm weird? Your dad's weird?"

"I'm serious, Mom," he said. "What am I supposed to say to her? What'll we talk about? I don't go to school. I don't go *any*where."

"Your problem is that you've never had a real friend, Sol," she said. "Give it a try, why don't you?"

"No way," he said, setting the letter down and walking back to his bedroom.

An hour later, Solomon was still lying on his floor staring up at the ceiling. Their house was built in the seventies, so it had that weird gold glitter mixed in the white popcorn plaster on its ceilings. Solomon liked to count the little shiny flecks, but never made it past a hundred before his eyes starting going blurry and they all seemed to blink and glow like they were real stars, like the roof had been ripped off his house and he could see them again.

He didn't really know if he wanted a friend. Some days were lonely, sure. Always quiet, but that was something he'd gotten used to a long time ago. And, like his mom said, he hadn't had a *real* friend in a long time, so what did he know about *being* one? Jack squat. That's what. He didn't fit in when he was in school, so how would he feel now, around someone whose life is out there where he's nothing but an alien? What he feared most was that all this hiding had made it impossible for him to ever be found again.

On top of that, Solomon was a little weirded out by the whole thing. He'd basically gotten a letter from his stalker and his mom was acting like they should be throwing a party over it. He didn't know if he could trust her on matters like this—when she could just be trying to push him closer to leaving the house again. His dad, though, always knew what to say.

"Dad," Solomon said, walking into the living room.

"There he is. Han Solo himself. Rebel without a cause."

"Mom tell you about the letter?"

"She read it to me."

"Sounds about right," Solomon said.

"Weird, huh?"

"So weird."

Solomon took a seat on the couch and picked the letter up off the coffee table. He read back over the first few lines before looking up at his dad with worry in his eyes.

"It's a quandary," his dad said. "On the one hand, she seems pretty genuine. On the other hand . . ."

"You shouldn't trust people who send letters to complete strangers asking to be their friends?"

"Exactly. But, your mom says you've got nothing to lose."

"Yeah, but, that's not true. I have a lot to lose. I like it here, Dad. The way it is. I get that I'm the only one who sees it that way, but can you guys at least try to understand that bringing someone else in here—changing everything— that it could make me go crazy again."

"You were never crazy. Don't say that."

Solomon knew very well that saying "crazy" was a sure way to make his dad get serious. Jason could insert a bad punch line into any conversation. Most of the time, Solomon loved this about his dad, but not when he was desperate for help.

"Tell me what to do, Dad. Please."

"Sleep on it," he said.

"I'm afraid I won't be able to."

"I don't know then, Sol. What would the robot do?"

"He's an android, but you're a genius, Dad," he said, getting up from his seat.

"You thought you got it from your mom?"

That android wasn't real, of course, but was the character Data from *Star Trek: The Next Generation* (or, *STTNG*). Solomon had seen every good episode of *STTNG* at least nine times, and every not-so-good episode three times or more, depending on how not-so-good it was. So he had a few ideas about where he could find some answers. And, yes, he got answers to a lot of life's questions from the show. When you only have your parents and your grandma to talk to, you figure out ways to learn about the world—and Solomon, for reasons that made terrific sense to him, had chosen a nineties space drama to forever be his compass.

After settling into his favorite chair with an alarming amount of candy, Solomon watched eight episodes in a row. It should be very obvious to you why Solomon would feel so deeply connected to Data, a character who, as an android, lived just on the edge of humanity. Because of this, Data always found a way to say something wise and painfully simple about existence and even before he stopped leaving the house, Solomon had proclaimed the character to be his personal hero.

When he was halfway through the eighth episode, Solomon found what he'd been looking for. In it, two characters are thought to be dead after a run-in with another ship. And there's this moment where Lt. Commander Data says that Geordi, one of the men feared dead, treated him just like he treated everyone else. He accepted him for what he was. And that, Data concluded, was true friendship.

Maybe he'd never realized it before, but, when Solomon heard it, he suddenly knew why Lisa Praytor scared the complete shit out of him. Because, like Data, he didn't want to be treated just as different as he was.

But, he already knew he was scared, so Data's wise words were only validation that he wasn't brave enough to invite Lisa over just yet. Maybe he needed someone wiser than Data, even though it pained him to admit it. He needed his grandmother. And, luckily, she was coming over for dinner. She wasn't like most grandmas, he was sure. For one thing, she was fairly young. She had Jason, her only child, when she was twenty. This was shortly after she'd left her small town in Louisiana to move out to Los Angeles and become an actress. One commercial and a Vegas wedding later, she'd gone from Hollywood hopeful to suburban housewife. And she loved it. Now, in her mid-sixties, she drove the sports car she'd always wanted and acted like the star she'd never become. She'd taken up selling real estate after Solomon's grandfather died in the eighties.

And by the time Solomon was born, she had an empire. And if he could leave the house, he'd see her face on signs in yards all over Upland.

"This is WONDERFUL!" she shouted immediately after reading the letter, her Southern accent peeking through every word.

"Wonderful?"

"Yes. Sounds like my kind of girl. She knows what she wants and she goes after it."

"But why would she want me? I mean, want to be friends with me?"

"Look at you. *I'd* be your friend if I didn't have one foot in the grave."

"You are my friend, Grandma."

"Well, there you go then."

"I don't think that helps me any," he said.

"Are you afraid it's a prank or something? Some punk ass punks trying to pull one over on you?"

"No," he said, laughing. "Don't say *punk ass punks*, Grandma."

"I know a lot of people in this town, Solomon. And a lot of their kids are spoiled little shits. It wouldn't surprise me one bit."

"No one even knows I exist."

"This girl does!" she said loudly. "So this is it then, Solomon? Just me, your parents, and the pizza guy for the rest of your life? You wanna stay in here all the time, that's fine by me. But at least let someone new in. If anything, it'll keep you from going completely nuts someday and killing us all."

"Is that what you think I'm going to do? Snap and kill you?" he asked.

"Not me, you won't. I keep mace in my purse. You never know what kind of creep'll be shopping for a house."

"Wait . . . what?"

"Invite her over, Sol. Do something different just to see what happens. Hell, I know I would. You get to be my age and you learn to start saying yes, even when you're a little scared."

"I'll think about it," he said. "Dad said to sleep on it."

"Your dad was a lonely little boy. Did you know that? He'd never tell you to think on it. He's just being nice."

"I'm not lonely."

"Not yet," she said. "But you're still young. It's going to get tougher and tougher the older you get. Nobody wants to come hang out with a middle-aged shut-in who lives with his parents."

"Geez, Grandma. Go easy on me, will you?"

"I'm just trying to help you here. Anyway, what else is new? What're you working on?"

She walked across his bedroom and flipped open his laptop. There were many things he wouldn't want his grandmother to find on his computer screen, and a website about swimming pools was, surprisingly, at the top of that list.

"Please don't tell them," he said. "Not yet."

"You want a pool?" she said, barely containing her excitement.

"Don't read into it, please. I just miss the water."

"This pool is *outside*, Solomon. How am I not supposed to be happy about this?"

She ran over and hugged him around the neck. He didn't move a muscle, waiting for her to let go and stop swaying from side to side. When she did, there were tears in her eyes.

"This is exactly why I'm not ready to show them yet," he said. "Too much pressure."

"I'll buy it, Solomon," she said. "Get them to say yes, and I'll build you the best pool in Upland."

"This doesn't mean I'll go out there," he said. "I mean, I want it to mean that, but I can't promise."

"You have to do one thing for me though, okay?" she said, raising an eyebrow.

"No," he said, shaking his head. "Really?"

"One visit," she said. "Let the poor girl come over for an afternoon and at least see if you like her. Either way, you get what you want. And what you *might* get is a friend to share that pool with."

She kissed him on the forehead and walked out of the room. When she got to the kitchen, Solomon could hear her as plain as day, like she'd never left his room. So, he listened for a while, making sure she wouldn't share his secret just yet. She was trustworthy, but sometimes her love of gossip got in the way of that. And he'd just given her the biggest piece of news to hit the Reed family in three years.

"Sol!" his mom yelled from the kitchen. "Phone!"

Solomon just sat there and stared at the phone sitting on his desk. Everyone he knew was right down the hall from him. So, who the hell was waiting for him to pick up?

"Hello?" he answered with hesitation.

"Solomon?" a girl's voice asked from the other end. "Is that you?"

"Yes."

"Lisa Praytor. Did you get my letter?"

Solomon held the phone away for a second and took three deep, calm breaths.

"Hello?" she said. "Are you there?"

"Here," he said, maybe too loudly. "I got your letter. Thank you."

"You're welcome." She sounded relieved and also really excited. "I hope it didn't, like, freak you out too bad or anything."

"Just a little," he said. "Not too much."

It had been a long time since Solomon had talked to someone this young, and he wasn't really sure what he was doing. He felt compelled to say things like "cool" and "chill" and "brb," and was very relieved that she was barely letting him speak.

"Anyway, I'm sorry to call like this, but I just wanted to confirm that you got the letter and that you know I am totally okay with whatever you decide. I will say this, though. I am a hell of a friend. You can ask my best friend Janis Plutko. Would you like her number?"

"No . . . thank you. I . . ."

"Oh no. I'm freaking you out *right now*, aren't I? I guess I just get too excited about things sometimes. Clark says I get too excited about everything. Even the things that piss me off. What sort of things piss you off, Solomon?"

"Umm . . . I don't know . . ."

"You know what? I'm sorry. I shouldn't have called. I have obviously caught you at a bad time. Would you like to call me later or . . ."

"Can you come over Wednesday?" he interrupted.

"This Wednesday? Of course I can."

"Great. So, the address is 125 Redding Way."

"Got it. How's after three p.m.? Are you free around then?"

"I'm always free," he answered. "So, yeah."

"Awesome. Thank you, Solomon. I promise this won't be weird. Just fun. Maybe a little weird, but weird in a fun way. *Fun*. Focus on the fun part."

"The fun part, right," he said. "I will."

"Until Wednesday then," she said.

"Okay. Bye."

He hung up and ran into the bathroom across the hall. He knelt down on the cold linoleum and stared into the toilet bowl. He could see his face in there, staring back at him as he drew in slow, deep breaths. Seeing himself in toilet water was *not* the way to feel confident about his decision to invite Lisa over. But, what could he do about that now anyway?

He didn't lose his lunch, but he came close. So he had to count and breathe and sit on the bathroom floor just in case it got worse. But it didn't. His heartbeat settled. The air got thicker. And he stood up. He walked over to the sink, splashed some water on his face, and then walked out into the hallway, letting it drip down his cheeks and neck, some of his hair stuck to his forehead.

Just before he stepped around the corner to the living room, he overheard his grandma spilling the beans about the pool, just like he knew she would. And as soon as he stepped into view, they all looked over at him in unison. Then he gave them an affirmative nod and they all smiled.

"Better buy this kid a bathing suit," Grandma said.

EIGHT

LISA PRAYTOR

Solomon didn't sound as wounded and frail as Lisa had expected. He sounded a little nervous, but no more so than anyone getting a phone call from a complete stranger would. Her first thought was relief—maybe this kid would be easier to help than she'd expected. But, she knew she couldn't assume too much before she'd even met him. And he said yes. She had no idea why anyone would get a phone call like that and actually agree to see her, but he had and he did and now she was well on her way to being the best thing that ever happened to him.

She wanted to share her good news with Clark, who was at his dad's apartment in Rancho Cucamonga where he spent a court-ordered fifty percent of his time. Harold Robbins was a tax attorney and he was just as boring as that sounds. But, he'd do anything for his kids and Lisa adored him. She called Clark and he picked up on the first ring.

"Clark Robbins, at your service."

"I'm in," she said.

"In what?"

"Solomon said yes. I'm going over Wednesday."

"Oh, wow. That's great."

"Yeah. I waited around all day for him to call, but then I decided I couldn't make it any longer."

"Wait . . . you called *him*? Lisa, the guy obviously wants to be left alone."

"Well, he took my call. And I figure he'd have hung up on me if he didn't want to hear what I had to say."

"Good point, I guess. Well, how'd he sound?"

"Normal," she said. "A little caught off guard, but why wouldn't he be?"

"So then you invited yourself over there?"

"No. Can you have a little more faith in me? It was his idea."

"So I'm supposed to feel better that another guy invited you over to his house?"

"Hmm . . . we're both making good points today."

"I'm serious, Lisa. You need to be careful."

"I'm always careful."

"You want to come over?" he asked, a little defeat in his voice. "You can spend some time with me before you meet your new boyfriend."

"Definitely. I need to study for a calculus test tomorrow, but I'd love an excuse to procrastinate."

"Sweet. We've got popcorn and Netflix. Bring candy."

"I'm not watching a war movie," she said firmly. "Otherwise, I'm headed over."

The next morning, after acing another test *and* being the first one in class to finish, Lisa spent her free period in the school library reading up on agoraphobia. She knew a little already—how it's pretty much just a result of panic disorder. And she knew Solomon would try to defend his choices, maybe argue that it's best for him, that reducing the stress of the outside world kept him healthy. And that was fine with her. But she believed there was a thin line between accepting one's fears and giving in to them altogether. And she was determined to help him overcome his. It wouldn't be easy, especially pretending to be his friend instead of his counselor, but she knew he'd thank her in the end, secret or no secret.

She also knew she couldn't go in and start cognitive behavioral therapy on the first day. She had to be subtle. This was a new kind of therapy anyway. It wasn't about counseling him back to health through endless conversations and waiting for tiny emotional breakthroughs. This was about giving him a friend who would, hopefully, make him want to try harder to get better. Her essay was about *her* experience with mental illness, after all, and if she could prove that her inventiveness, compassion, and patience were enough to help someone like Solomon, then maybe the people at Woodlawn would pick her. She was certain she'd be the only candidate smart enough to pull something like this off. Who knows, maybe they'd just hand her a degree and let her start grad school early.

"What're you doing?" Janis said, sneaking up behind her.

"Oh, hey. Just some research for my history paper."

To avoid being talked out of it, and to respect his privacy, Lisa wasn't going to tell Janis about Solomon. Did she feel a little guilty for being secretive? Maybe. But she was way too determined to make this essay thing work to listen to another one of Janis's lectures on morality.

"Boring," Janis said. "You want to hang out after school?"

"Can't. I'm helping Clark's sister with her geometry homework."

"Is she paying you?"

"Clark's dad is. Ten bucks an hour."

"Damn," Janis said. "I mean, *darn*."

Lisa knew helping Solomon would probably put a strain on her friendship with Janis. She knew it would eat up time with Clark, too, not to mention all the hours she needed for studying, working on the yearbook layout, *and* presiding over Student Council meetings once, sometimes twice, a week. But it was worth it. Some people sign on for the impossible. And they're the ones everybody remembers.

She'd seen his house before—not because she was stalking him or anything—but because she'd been to a birthday party across the street once as a kid. When she got out of her car, an orange cat darted across the driveway and made her jump a little, almost dropping the cookies she'd baked for Solomon in the process. Yes, she'd baked him cookies.

"Look!" she blurted out nervously as soon as he opened the door, presenting the plastic-wrapped plate with her arms outstretched. "Cookies!"

"Hi," he said.

He was standing several feet back, but he leaned forward to take the cookies and she got her first good look at

him. He was handsome. His dark hair was slicked back to
one side and he had big brown eyes—the kind that look a
little green sometimes in the right light. He was tall, too,
much taller than she'd expected. At least 6'1". He smiled
at her after he spoke, but she could immediately see how
unnerved he was by all of this.

"That your cat?" she asked, still standing outside.

"Oh, no. That's Fred. He's the neighbors'."

"Ah. I'm allergic."

"Same here." He nodded his head a little.

"Solomon? Am I going to get to come inside?"

"Yeah . . . yeah . . . sorry. God. Come on in."

He stepped back away from the door and let her enter.
Then he used one foot to gently kick it shut, and Lisa wondered if that was as close as he'd get to the outside.

"So . . . umm . . ." Solomon attempted. "I don't really . . ."

"Give me a tour?" she interrupted. "That'd be a good
place to start maybe."

"Right, right," he said. "Uh . . . this is the foyer, I guess."

"It's lovely," she said.

He showed her the living room, dining room, kitchen,
and den without saying much more. She asked lots of
questions though, and he gave the shortest answers he
could muster.

"Do you cook much?" she asked.

"Not really."

"Is that your Xbox?"

"No, it's my dad's."

"Can I see your room?"

"Sure."

In his room, with its bright white, empty walls, Solomon took a seat on the edge of the bed and watched as Lisa walked around, inspecting his bookshelves and the tchotchkes he had scattered around on his desk. She was trying to be nonchalant, but it was hard to do with him watching her like that.

"You like to read I see."

"Passes the time."

"Yeah. I guess it would."

"Lisa," he said, "can I ask you something?"

"Sure." She sat down in his desk chair.

"Why are you here?"

"You know the answer to that," she said. "To be your friend. But you're going to have to be a little more talkative to keep up with me."

"Sorry," he said. "I'm not really sure what to talk about."

"You wanna start by explaining these walls? It looks like a hospital room in here."

He laughed. And *when* he laughed, Lisa took her first full breath since walking through the door.

"I just like it that way, I guess."

"Minimalist."

"Huh?"

"*Minimalist*," she repeated. "Very trendy right now, actually."

"Oh," he said with a shrug. "Lots of stuff makes me feel closed in."

"You'd hate my house," she said. "My mom can't stand an empty wall. If she had good taste in art, that might be okay. But it's all roosters and cheap landscapes from

Wal-Mart. She had a cow print phase a few years ago that I almost didn't survive."

Another laugh. She was definitely sensing that he was starting to appreciate her humor. And he seemed a little less anxious than when she'd arrived. Complete sentences were a good sign.

"I think maybe it's because I'm inside so much," he said. "I guess I like the idea of my room seeming endless or something."

"Yeah," she said. "I like that. Or maybe you could just imagine whatever you want in here."

"No," he said. "That's what the garage is for."

"Oh. Okay."

A few minutes later, as he opened the door that led from the laundry room into the garage, he looked at Lisa with a very serious expression and then let the door slowly open and stood to one side. She stepped through the threshold, and he watched her without saying another word.

The entire garage had been painted a deep, solid black and was covered with a bright yellow grid. It was one of the strangest things Lisa had ever seen, and she had no idea what she was looking at.

"Have you ever seen *Star Trek: The Next Generation*?" he asked, walking to the center of the room.

"A couple times," she said. "My boyfriend watches it. I sort of wish everyone on earth had Patrick Stewart's voice."

"Your lips to God's ears."

She shut the door behind her to find that even *it* had been painted to match the pattern of the room. Square after square of blackness, highlighted with these intersecting beams that covered not just the floor and walls, but also the ceiling.

"This is my version of a holodeck," he said. "On the show. Well, on several versions of *Star Trek*, they use a room like this for simulated reality. Training, to solve puzzles, things like that. It's nice, right?"

She was a little caught off guard that he was suddenly speaking to her so casually, the nerves in his voice barely noticeable anymore. As someone who worked very hard to get the things she wanted in life, this was a level of devotion that Lisa could appreciate. And all she could think about was how much Clark would love it.

"So, then, what do you do in here?"

"Well, I come in here, I sit down in the middle of the floor, and I just think stuff up to entertain myself. They say using your imagination makes you live longer."

"They *do* say that," she agreed. "So, you just think stuff up and picture it happening all around you?"

"Sure," he said. "You don't ever do that? Imagine being somewhere else?"

"I think about being in college," she said. "All the time, actually. Far away from Upland."

"Yeah, so, it's like that. Except the college part. I don't think that's in my future."

"You never know."

"Yes you do," he confirmed. "What do you want to study?"

"Medicine," she answered. "Not sure what kind yet, but being Dr. Praytor is definitely part of the dream."

"No wonder my mom likes you so much."

"Can I try?" she asked, walking over to the center of the room and sitting down.

"Oh . . . umm . . . sure."

"What do I do?" she asked.

He walked over and sat down beside her. This was the closest they'd gotten, their knees nearly touching, and she could tell it made him tense up a little.

"Okay. Close your eyes," he said. "I mean, if you want to."

So she closed her eyes, and it was so quiet in the room that she could hear his breathing.

"Okay. Now open them," he said. And she did. And she saw a black room with yellow squares covering it and a teenage boy staring at her in the dark with a grin on his face.

"What?" she asked.

"Do you see it?"

"See what?"

"We're in a field. It's so green. All around us. And there's a kite in the air. You see it?" He pointed up toward the ceiling.

She looked up, seeing nothing but the same yellow squares from corner to corner and then looked his way. He was mesmerized by the room around them. His expression like Heaven had opened up to swallow the Earth. Was this guy for real? Kites? She wasn't scared of him, not at all. She was just suddenly realizing that maybe she couldn't help him.

"Lisa?"

"Yeah," she answered.

"I'm just fucking with you."

And he was. The holodeck garage wasn't a place for him to imagine elaborate settings and interact with fictional people or anything. It was a garage painted to look like something he loved. And *that*, in and of itself, was all he needed it to be. Just a place to escape when closing his eyes wasn't enough. Sometimes, like after the panic attack he'd had a few days before, it was the only way he could block it all out and try to reset his thoughts.

"That's not funny," she said, holding back a nervous laugh.

"The grid's actually yellow tape," he said. "Took forever."

"Oh wow," she said, feeling the tape with her fingertips. "You bring every girl you meet to this creepy room?"

"*That* is funny," he said, hopping up from the floor and reaching a hand down to hoist her up.

"Thanks."

"Sorry," he said.

Solomon and his family had a shorthand way of showing their affection for one another and it usually involved poking fun at even the most serious things. Just the week before, he called his dad a "dork" and was met with a simple and quick "recluse" and thought nothing of it. They were just like this—smart enough to make fun of themselves before anyone could beat them to it.

"No worries," she said, nudging his arm.

It was only her elbow and only for a quick second, but it still felt foreign and strange and exciting to him. And, without even realizing it, he gently held the spot on his arm where she'd done it as they walked out into the living room.

"Thanks for the tour," she said.

"Please stop by the gift shop on your way out."

"You sound like Clark."

"I guess that's your boyfriend?" he asked.

"Yeah. Been together a while now."

"I didn't think I could remind anyone of anyone."

Lisa laughed and shook her head. "It's a compliment, of course."

"What's he like? I'm betting he doesn't have a holodeck."

"Well, he's a water polo player. Smart but not a know-it-all. His mom's a nightmare, but his dad's cool. They're divorced. He's tall, but just a little shorter than you, I think. The season just ended and he's depressed about it or something because he's been, like, flaking a lot lately . . . with everyone but me. I tried talking to him about it, but he doesn't like to get too serious. It's a problem, really, but I'm working on it."

"Okay . . . that was a *lot* of information on Clark. Got it."

"Also, he hides his comic books under his bed when his friends come over. How stupid is that?"

Lisa clicked around on her phone and handed it to him. It was a picture of her and Clark, in formal wear, taken at some school dance or something.

"Tell me why someone who looks like *that* would ever be embarrassed of anything."

"No clue," Solomon said quickly, barely glancing at the screen. "Looks like the king of high school to me. I'd die there, wouldn't I?"

"You watch too much TV," she said. "High school isn't what you think it is."

"Isn't it a little, though? He hides his comics."

"So, maybe a little," she said. "But you'd be okay at it, I bet."

"Is there a fountain?" he asked with a half-serious expression.

"You're very different from what I expected, Solomon Reed."

"I hope that's a good thing."

"Absolutely."

He was glad she didn't stay too much longer because, despite having had a good time, all that talking and trying to come up with new things to say or questions to ask was making his head hurt. Then, as soon as he shut the door behind her, he started to feel like he couldn't catch his breath. He leaned against the wall for a second, trying to breathe through it, hoping he could shake it off. But he couldn't. Now hyperventilating, he stumbled down the hallway and into his bedroom, where he crawled under the covers and rode it out, his body shaking from side to side, his eyes closed so tightly they were starting to hurt. It was brief but intense, and afterward Solomon just lay there listening to his breath as it leveled out. Sometimes that's all you can do when it happens—hold on just long enough for the world to stop shaking. There's a reason people mistake them for heart attacks and every time it happened to Solomon, a little part of him wondered if maybe his chest would explode. Other times, he wondered if that would make it all better.

"So . . . how'd it go?" his mom asked when she got home from work.

"Good," he answered. "She's nice."

"Solomon," she said sternly, "use your words. It's all I could think about today. I should've just stayed home. How you talked us into leaving you alone for this, I will never . . ."

"Sorry," he interrupted. "Yeah . . . she came over and I showed her around. We just talked a little. No biggie, Mom."

"Did you show her the garage?"

"Maybe."

"That may be something you want to ease your friends into."

"*Friends?* Mom, don't blow this out of proportion. Who knows if I'll ever even see her again?"

"I don't care about that," she said. "What's important is whether or not you *want* to see her again."

Solomon thought about that for the rest of the night. He'd already given his parents so much more hope than they'd had in a long time just by seeing Lisa. So now he had two choices: He could refuse to see her again and break their hearts, or he could keep going along with this whole *friend* thing and see what would happen.

The next morning, he woke up to what he thought was the world ending. He'd imagined it before—watching from his window as flames fell from the sky with the news on loud in the background and neighbors screaming, maybe even his parents running into the room to hug him one last time. But he'd never imagined it to be quite so loud, with a roaring coming from all directions. Maybe it was an earthquake, he decided, jumping out of bed and running over to stand in the doorway. He waited there for a minute, the adrenaline waking him up with every nervous blink of his eyes, and eventually realized that the house wasn't even shaking.

He ran out to the living room and before he could even get to the sliding glass doors leading to the backyard, he could see what was going on. There was a bulldozer digging a very large hole behind his house.

"No way," he said aloud.

There was no going back now, was there? He had very few surprises in his life and this one hit him hard. He took a seat on the edge of the couch and leaned forward, letting his head hang between his legs. He covered his ears and closed his eyes and let himself sway a little on the balls of his feet. Maybe there wasn't an earthquake, but the world still vibrated and shook all around him. His thoughts stabbed him like knives and suddenly his shoulders were so heavy he could hardly keep from falling all the way down to the floor. He gasped for air, his lungs never getting full enough to satisfy him. If someone had been home, they would've heard it, the sound of someone suffocating on his own breath. It sounded like he was dying, and it felt that way, too.

He composed himself after a few minutes, grabbing a glass of water in the kitchen and taking a seat at the counter. His thoughts still spiraled, and his body ached with a lack of energy that only came after a sudden attack like this. Could he go out there for them? Would he be able to go outside without freaking out? Would it kill him?

Then he thought about Lisa. She had no idea what she meant to them, did she? She probably felt like some stranger invading their personal space and she definitely *was*, but she could very well end up saving them all. And what the hell was he supposed to do if she didn't want to come back? What if just a little over an hour with him was enough to satisfy her curiosity? He wouldn't be surprised one bit if she never showed up again, and now he felt bad about *that,* too.

Around lunchtime, Solomon was doing his schoolwork at the kitchen counter and watching the backyard with one eye. A couple of times, he made eye contact with a few of the crew guys and immediately put his head down like it had never happened. He didn't like these strangers walking around in his backyard, right there where he could see them from all angles of the living room and kitchen. This was his inner sanctum, and it was being violated by loud machines and strangers in work boots.

He thought about going to the garage, but the one little dim lightbulb wasn't enough to solve matrices under.

He settled on his dad's office, figuring it would be quiet enough if he shut the door. Then, as soon as he got started, he was interrupted by the telephone. He only ever answered it if his parents were calling or if he recognized the number. But, despite that not being the case, Solomon had a feeling that it was Lisa Praytor. So he picked up.

"Hello."

"Solomon!" Lisa said with a burst of enthusiasm.

"Hello," he repeated.

"What's up? Me? I'm currently skipping study hall to make photocopies for a Student Council fund-raiser. *This* is my life."

"Oh," he said. "I'm just . . . doing homework actually."

"Oh, yeah? I didn't even think about that. I guess it's all homework for you, right?"

"Right," he said.

"Look, umm, what're your plans on Saturday night?"

"Lisa, we've been over this."

"Right," she chuckled. "So, you want some company?"

"Are you serious? Yeah, sure. I mean . . . there's not much to do around here."

"There are no boring places, only boring people," she said with confidence.

"All right," he said.

"Great. Be there around six if that works for you."

"Of course," he said.

"Great. See you then, Solomon Reed."

"Bye."

So she wanted to come back. A real-live teenage girl who could've spent her time doing all sorts of normal teenage things with other normal teenagers wanted to come hang out with Solomon Reed on a Saturday night. It was enough to make his stomach start gurgling and his head get a little woozy. There was no denying it. Now he knew it to be absolutely true: He had a friend. And he was terrified of her.

TEN

LISA PRAYTOR

As a freshman, Lisa had taken and passed the only AP psychology course at Upland High School. In fact, she scored higher on the exam than anyone else in the class of mostly juniors and seniors. But, it was simply an introduction to the field of psychology and not nearly enough to qualify Lisa as any sort of psychological expert. She was only seventeen by a few months. But, she believed in herself maybe more than other people believed in God or the devil or Heaven or Hell. She knew she was right. And she didn't need a textbook to prove it. Now, with her second session with Solomon on the books, she was feeling more confident than ever that she could get him out of that house and get herself out of Upland.

After school on Friday, she ran home to change clothes and grab a snack before heading over to Clark's. She didn't expect to see her mother, but her car was in the driveway when she pulled up. Her mom worked a lot, and when she wasn't working, she tried to spend as little time as possible at home. Lisa figured she either hated her or hated Ron the stepdad. Either way, she was there today, on a weekday afternoon before five, and it was weird. When Lisa walked in, she saw dirty dishes on the counter by the sink and heard the television at an ungodly volume coming from the den. She tried to sneak through without being heard, but her mom was yelling her name by the time she got to the refrigerator.

"Lisa!" she shouted from the living room. "Is that you?"

"Yes, Mom."

"Come here, honey!"

She walked around the corner to find her mother lying on the couch, a big fluffy quilt covering her all the way to the chin. Lisa couldn't remember the last time she'd seen her mom during a workday.

"Are you okay?" she asked her, picking up the remote and muting the TV.

"Just nursing a cold, sweetie," she said. "Talk to me. I'm lonely."

Lisa took a seat across from her on the recliner that was usually reserved for Ron the stepdad. Ron hadn't been around for days though, so Lisa wasn't sure what was going on. They *did* fight a lot and it wouldn't surprise her to find out that he'd left for good this time. Just like Tim the stepdad did two years before. And Lisa could tell the difference between sick and sad.

"A cold, huh?"

"Don't talk back, Lisa."

"That wasn't talking back," she defended. "Where's Ron?"

"Business trip. At least that's what he told me."

"Do you think he's lying or something?" Lisa asked.

"I just don't know anymore."

Then she started crying. She always cried when she talked about Ron. Lisa had stopped feeling sorry for her a long time ago. But she still sat there and listened as her mom went on and on about a fight they'd had the night before. It was over money this time, which didn't surprise Lisa one bit. Her mom worked eighty hours a week and Ron had been changing jobs a lot lately, which wasn't a good sign. Do phlebotomists even take business trips?

"I'm sure everything will be fine," Lisa said.

"I know, honey. You know how emotional I get sometimes. I just need a good cry and then I'll be back to normal."

But Lisa wondered whose definition of *normal* her mother was going by. Things with her mom had always been weird. And she didn't have the world's best track record for maintaining healthy relationships, either. In fact, that was the longest conversation she'd had with her daughter in months.

Eventually, Lisa was able to go change clothes and when she got back downstairs, her mom was asleep. She cleaned the dishes and took out the trash. She wrote a note saying she'd be at Clark's. And then she set a glass of water and two aspirins on the coffee table next to her mom on her way out.

When she got to Clark's, he was in the driveway playing basketball with his little sister. Drew was only thirteen to

Clark's seventeen, but she was nearly as tall and a much better basketball player.

"Why even bother, Drew?" Lisa asked once out of her car.

"Right?" she said, shooting the ball.

"Hey, hey," Clark said. "I'm letting her win."

He walked over to hug Lisa and she held on for a little longer than usual, despite how playing basketball in the spring made him smell.

"Better save him, Lisa," Drew said. "This game's getting ugly."

They went upstairs to Clark's room and, as soon as the door was shut, Lisa started kissing him. It was pretty much the same every time. He would kiss her like they were filming a scene in a movie or something, all passion and no restraint. And then as soon as things started to heat up, he'd ease off and kiss her like they were at a middle school dance in the fifties. And God forbid Lisa tried to put her hands below his waist. He would, in the nicest and most subtle way possible, move her hands right back up to his stomach or chest every single time. And his stomach and chest, while quite impressive, could only do so much for Lisa.

"I love you," he said before a long kiss.

"I love you, too," she said back, again with her hands moving down.

"Come on, quit it."

"You quit," she said, trying again.

"Lisa!" he yelled, jumping up.

She was too embarrassed to say anything, so she just

fell back onto the bed, grabbed a pillow, and held it over her face. She thought she might cry, but she didn't do that often and it always took more out of her than it was worth.

"Lisa? Babe?" Clark said gently, sitting beside her and rubbing her arm. "I'm so sorry. I didn't mean to act like that."

"Do you need to tell me something, Clark? Is there something I'm doing wrong?" she asked, her voice muffled by the pillow.

"No. No, not at all. Look, it's just . . . I can't *wait* to do this with you. But I told you I'm not ready. And I'm trying not to let the embarrassment kill me."

She sat up, letting the pillow fall to one side. It looked like he'd been crying, or close to it anyway. She'd never made him cry before, never even seen it. She'd seen her stepdad cry though. It was something her mom had a strange talent for—turning a fight into a shame-fest that always ended with Ron getting emotional. Lisa didn't remind herself of her mother very often, so this made her squirm and sent a sharp pain shooting through her stomach.

"Clark . . . I . . ." she said with a sad smile. "It's okay. I'm sorry."

She leaned forward to hug him, and he let his forehead rest on her shoulder. He was breathing so hard. She let the tip of her nose touch his and then she closed her eyes.

"What're you doing?" he asked.

"Ancient meditation ritual," she whispered. "Repeat after me."

"Okay," he whispered back.

"Lisa is the only thing that matters," she said in an almost chant. "Lisa is my life. She is queen of all that is good."

"You say this to yourself?" he asked, holding in a laugh.

"Self-esteem is very important."

"Let's take a nap," Clark said, holding her tightly. "The queen must rest."

She wasn't sure how long they'd been asleep, but it was definitely dark out and Clark's family was definitely home. She could hear his mom's voice downstairs, probably talking to Drew.

"Clark," she whispered. "Wake up."

"What time is it?" he asked.

She got her phone off the bedside table, and the light from the screen nearly blinded them both. Seven thirteen p.m.

"Shit," she said. "Your *mom*. Get up. Shit shit shit."

"It's okay. Maybe she's not home yet."

"I can hear her. Now *get up* and help me sneak out."

"She doesn't care," he said. "I promise."

Out of all the times Lisa had come over after school like this, she'd never stayed long enough to see Patty Robbins home from work. She'd always just assumed that they'd both get into big trouble if they were caught upstairs in his room with the door shut. His mom was a churchgoer, after all, and Lisa figured teenage sex wasn't high on her list of Jesus-approved activities.

"Oh my God." She walked over to the window, looking down into the backyard.

"Your car's out front, Lisa," he said. "She already knows you're here anyway."

"Shit."

She gave him a blank stare and started putting her socks and shoes on. Then she tied her hair up and tried to compose herself.

"This is so embarrassing," she said. "What do we do?"

"MOM!" Clark shouted.

"What the hell?" Lisa whispered.

She could feel her cheeks turning a warm red. A few seconds later, Patty Robbins poked her head through the door. "Yeah, hon?"

"Lisa's here. We took a nap."

"Oh. Hi, Lisa. Great. Stay for dinner?"

"S . . . sure," she managed.

"Taco Thursday!" she said loudly, vanishing from sight.

"I told her it's supposed to be Taco Tuesday, but she won't listen," Clark said.

Lisa took a seat on the bed and started laughing.

"I was so scared," she said, slapping Clark on the arm.

"We work under complete transparency here."

"What do you mean?"

"She trusts me," he answered, shrugging his shoulders.

And why wouldn't she? He's had his girlfriend in his bedroom alone countless times now and had, every single time, failed to seal the deal. Lisa shook her head and looked at him. He was too nice to be mad at, which sometimes drove her absolutely insane. But not tonight. She didn't want to fight. She just wanted to have dinner with his nice little normal family.

Lisa stayed for a while after, watching TV with Clark and Drew and wondering how late she'd have to stay out to avoid running into her mother again. Around eleven o'clock, she decided she'd better head home, so Clark walked her out to her car.

"So, movie this Saturday? Something scary?" he asked, leaning down outside of her car window.

"Oh," she said. "Umm . . . I sort of have plans, actually."

"Plans? What kind of plans?"

"Solomon," she said with her teeth clenched.

"Solomon . . ." he said slowly.

"Seriously? Are you upset because I . . ."

"I'm just . . . I guess I'm not really sure what to do with myself now."

"Now? Clark, this isn't going to be every weekend. I promise."

"I want you to be up front with me," he said.

"Of course."

"Anything I need to worry about with this guy? Because you say it's for your essay thing, but it seems weird that you're already going back over there."

"You have nothing to worry about," she said. "I don't think he swings my way, if you know what I mean."

"Convenient."

"Don't be like that," she said. "I've told him all about you. Nothing to worry about."

"Try to see it from my side, Lisa."

"Well, maybe you can meet him eventually," she said. "He's into *Star Trek*. Did I tell you that?"

"No," he said, turning her way, excitement in his eyes. *"Next Generation?"*

"Yep."

"I take it all back," he said. "This guy sounds amazing."

"He's . . . interesting. But, nice. And funny, too. I didn't think he'd be funny."

"Do you think *I'm* funny?" Clark asked.

"Funny looking," she said.

"Please. I bet you dream about this face at night."

"Yep," she played along. "My dreams are just your face with lasers shooting out of the eyes."

"Awesome."

"Anyway, let me make sure he isn't a complete psychopath first and I'll figure out a good time to introduce you guys."

"He hasn't left his house in three years, Lisa. He's not crazy. He's a genius. Just TV and video games twenty-four/seven. I think he's my new hero."

"Who was your old one?"

"Well, there's this old guy at the Vons on Foothill who greets you when you walk in. I think he was probably the one to beat until now."

"You're so weird. The grocery store greeter is your hero?"

"Was my hero. Pay attention."

It struck her on the way home that maybe she could use Clark's jealousy to her benefit. She figured most of it was playful enough, but if she could get him over there, it would only raise her chances of getting Solomon better— and it may even speed up the process. His therapy, after all, was about showing him that the world wasn't the scary, chaotic place he remembered it being. And Lisa knew introducing him to Clark Robbins was maybe the best way to prove that not everything out here is so bad.

ELEVEN
SOLOMON REED

There were no two ways about it—he was going to have to tell her. Which would be his first time ever saying it aloud. Solomon was gay. He'd realized it sometime around the age of twelve. It wasn't a hard thing to figure out, really. He saw boys and girls differently. And he preferred seeing one to the other. It's simple like that when you're young. And Solomon was sure it would always be that simple for him—why would he ever need to acknowledge his sexuality if he didn't ever plan on leaving the house again?

But he'd have to tell Lisa because now, with this Saturday night sort-of-date, Solomon was entertaining the possibility that he'd somehow struck a romantic chord with his new friend. He didn't know any better, really. He was handsome enough. And his mom had made sure he combed his hair before Lisa's first visit. So maybe he *had* charmed her in just one short afternoon. He'd surprised even himself with all his joking around and talking. Isn't that mostly what couples do together anyway? Don't they

just act goofy and talk and then take breaks for sex and
stuff?

What he couldn't reconcile, though, was why Lisa
would ever choose him over Clark Robbins. He'd seen the
picture on her phone, and he knew good and well that no
girl in her right mind would opt out of being with that guy
for a reclusive borderline albino who didn't even own a
pair of shoes. So maybe he was being paranoid. Maybe he
was reading way too much into her friendliness.

"What're you kids going to watch? Nothing rated *R* I
hope," his dad asked Saturday evening as they waited for
Lisa to arrive.

Solomon was lying faceup on the living room floor,
staring at the ceiling and listening to the TV.

"I can't decide," he answered. "Nothing sci-fi."

"Why's that?"

"Well, she's seen the garage. I don't want her thinking
I'm one-dimensional."

"Why do *you* care?" his dad asked in that nosy-parental
tone he used sometimes.

"That's a very good question, Dad."

Solomon stood up as soon as he heard the doorbell. But
once he was on his feet, he nearly fell back down. It had
come on as quickly as any he'd ever had—a sudden flush
in his cheeks, an unstoppable throbbing in his chest. He
leaned against the wall with one whole side of his body
and focused on counting. If you can get to ten, he thought,
you can breathe. And he did. And he breathed.

"Dad," he said between breaths.

"Shit," his dad said, hopping up and running over to him. "C'mon. Let's go back to your room."

His mom walked out from the kitchen when the doorbell rang for the second time and, without asking, knew exactly what was going on. So, she planted a big smile on her face and opened the door.

"Lisa!"

"Hi," Lisa said, stepping inside.

"He'll be out in a minute. I think he's probably trying to comb his hair or something," she said with an amused look on her face. "Have a seat and I'll go check."

She walked down the hallway and into her son's room. He was sitting on the bed, his dad beside him, leaning forward a little with his eyes closed. He was breathing. He was counting. He would be okay, but that didn't make it any easier to see him like this. It was never easy for them.

"Should I ask her to go?" his mom asked.

"No," Solomon managed, his eyes still closed.

When Valerie returned to the living room, Lisa was sitting on the couch and leaning over to look at a framed photograph on the side table.

"Big Bear Lake," Valerie said. "We used to have a cabin up there. I bet we went at least once a month."

"I love Big Bear."

"I really miss it," she said. "Cold weather always suited me better."

"I like the mountains," Lisa said. "It's about the only thing Upland has going for it."

"More like hills," Valerie added. "He'll be out in a minute."

"Everything okay?"

"Oh yes. Last time I checked, he was trying to find a pair of matching socks."

"*I* can't even do that," Lisa said, immediately realizing how insensitive it sounded. "Sorry . . . I didn't mean it like . . ."

"Hush," Valerie interrupted before pausing for a few long, quiet seconds. "I'm not naive, Lisa. Sol's unique. He can't find matching socks because he probably hasn't worn them since the last time he left the house and, by my count, that was a long damn time ago."

Lisa smiled at her, but stayed quiet. Then Valerie laughed a little to herself as she took a seat on the sofa. Suddenly, her mood shifted and she scooted up to rest her elbows on her knees before speaking to Lisa in a whisper.

"Tell me something," she said. "Do you like him?"

"What do you mean?" Lisa asked.

"Solomon. Do you like him? Is he *likable*?"

"Yeah. Totally."

"You're not lying, right? And don't try to spare my feelings. Solomon's never gotten away with a lie in his life."

"It's the truth," Lisa defended. "I was afraid he'd be boring."

"It's important that you know something, Lisa."

"Okay."

"I've been really scared—about Solomon and all the time he spends alone and in this house. And then you come along and suddenly he's talking about swimming and getting a tan. I don't know if it's crazy to believe him or not. But we couldn't dig that pool any faster if we tried."

"You're getting a pool?" Lisa asked, looking over toward the windows that face out into the backyard.

"He said he wanted one," she answered. "He said he'd go outside."

"No way."

"I need you to promise me something, Lisa."

"Okay."

"Promise me you'll stick around for as long as it takes to get him out there. That's all I'm asking. If you get bored or just decide he's not the kind of friend you wanted him to be—just please wait until we can get him out there, okay?"

"Okay," Lisa said. "But, I . . ."

"Thank you," she interrupted.

Just as she was about to ask more about the pool, Solomon stepped into the room and said "Hello."

He was visibly unnerved, but no more so than the first time she'd come over. He was wearing a T-shirt and shorts, with no socks. Lisa looked right at his bare feet and over to his mom.

"Okay. You guys can have the living room. I've got to run up to the office and . . . Sol, where's your dad?"

"Right here," Jason said, walking in. "Hi, Lisa. I'm Jason."

Lisa stood up and they shook hands. He looked over to Solomon and smiled, giving him a wink.

"All right, let's get out of their hair. Nobody wants two old people hanging around," his mom said.

"I do," Solomon joked nervously. "Tell us about taxes."

"And what exactly *is* a 401k?" Lisa added.

Jason and Valerie walked out of the room, still laughing. Lisa sat down at one end of the sofa and Solomon sat at the opposite end, an entire cushion length between them. He flipped through movies on the TV screen in silence, never looking her way.

"You get shy on me, Sol?" Lisa asked.

"Sorry."

"It's cool. Got something in mind?"

"Not really," he said. "I can't be trusted with this. Here, take it."

"Okay," she said, reaching over to grab the remote from him. "So, let's be smart about this. Comedy, sci-fi, drama, or horror?"

"No sci-fi," he said promptly, sticking to his guns.

"Deal."

"Your turn," he said.

"Oh . . . umm . . . no drama."

"Great. No horror. I hate scary movies."

"Me too. Clark makes me watch them and then I can't sleep for a week."

"That's actually spousal abuse," he joked. "Okay, comedy then."

"Thank God," she said. "What makes *you* laugh, Solomon Reed?"

"I don't know . . . slapstick?"

"I knew it," she said. "I know this is old school, but are you a fan of Mel Brooks?"

A huge smile stretched across his face.

"Where'd you come from?" he asked her.

"Upland," she said. "Keep up, will you? I vote *Robin Hood: Men in Tights*."

"Is my mom paying you to be here?"

"No," she said, scanning the screen for the movie. "But I *do* like to swim. And, you know, a free root canal would be nice, should the occasion ever arise."

"She told you about the pool, I guess."

"She did. And you're going to swim in that pool, yeah?"

"That's right," he answered.

"She seems pretty psyched," Lisa said. "That you asked for it, I mean."

"No pressure," he said. "Did she tell you my grandma bribed me?"

"No she did not. How so?"

"Said she'd buy the pool if I hung out with you."

"Smart," Lisa said before getting really quiet.

"Just the first time," he said. "Not anymore. I want you here."

"Oh good. I was getting scared this situation would forever ruin *Robin Hood: Men in Tights* for me."

"That would be tragic," he said. "I think my grandma's hoping you'll fall in love with me and save me from myself."

"Too bad I've got Clark," she joked.

"Too bad I'm gay," he blurted out, closing his eyes and expecting the silence to be deafening.

"Yeah, too bad," she said with a big smile.

She raised her hand into the air for a high five and he sort of just looked at it until she put it back down.

"I've never told anyone before."

"Oh my God," she said. "Thank you."

"For being gay or for telling you?"

"Both?"

"You're welcome. I sort of had a panic attack when you got here."

"I figured. Your mom said you were trying to find socks."

"She's a bad liar," he said, raising his foot into the air and wiggling his toes.

"At least give her credit for trying. She seems really cool."

"Pretty cool," he agreed. "Dad too. This wouldn't really work if they weren't, I guess."

"And, umm . . . do *they* know? That you're gay?"

"Why waste their time with it? It's not like it'll ever be an issue anyway."

"Yeah, but, it's who you are, right?"

"I guess so," he said. "I don't really know how to be any way else."

"When did you know?"

"I was twelve maybe. Something I just knew one day, even though I hadn't known it the day before."

"So it's like that, huh? A feeling? Not just being into other dudes?"

"Oh no, it's *that* too. Of course it's that. But it's more, I think. Not so much a feeling as a fact, like having blue eyes or brown hair. It's just maybe something you don't discover until you're ready to understand it better."

"Like being straight," she said. "Only we don't have to deal with all that closet bullshit."

"Bingo," he said.

She slipped off her shoes, and put her feet up with his.

"Oh," he said, standing up. "I have candy."

"Make it happen, Cap'n," she said.

When he got back from the kitchen, a box of Mike and Ike's in one hand and Hot Tamales in the other, he sat much closer to her, so close their elbows occasionally grazed during the entire movie. And like they'd done it a million times, without even thinking about it, they silently passed the candy back and forth between them with their eyes locked on the screen.

TWELVE
LISA PRAYTOR

L isa ended up staying at Solomon's house until well after midnight. Then, just as they were about to say good-bye at the front door, she asked if she could give him a hug.

"Sure," he whispered. "But make it quick."

She didn't. She held on just long enough for him to know she meant it. And she did mean it. He had told her something he'd never told anyone else in his entire life. If that isn't friendship, then what is? She was in the inner circle now. Hell, she *was* the inner circle. And all the progress she'd made in just two visits with Solomon was enough to help her ignore that little pang of guilt she was feeling in her stomach.

"You can tell Clark, too," he said before she left. "He should probably know he's got nothing to worry about."

Even though it was one in the morning before she got home, she needed to talk to Clark. He was at his dad's again, so she knew he'd be up late eating junk food and playing video games or something. And he was.

"Yellow," he answered. She could hear a TV in the background.

"Well, you don't have to be jealous of Solomon anymore."

"Bad date?" he joked.

"He's definitely gay."

"Oh. Funny."

"Funny?"

"Not funny *ha-ha*, but, you know, funny like *my girl-friend's other boyfriend is gay*."

"Shut up," she said. "Anyway. I just wanted you to know."

"Great. I'll alert my mom. She'll have some bibles mailed over ASAP."

"It's nothing to joke about, Clark."

"Sorry. I think it's great he told you. Sounds like he needed someone to talk to."

"I guess so," she said. "He asked his parents for a pool."

"He goes outside? I'm confused."

"No. But he says he's going to."

"Crazy," he said. "But not like *crazy* crazy. You know what I mean."

"It was sort of sad," she said. "He told me he isn't sure he'll ever tell his parents. Says it's a nonissue."

"He's not wrong, is he? If he never leaves the house, what's it matter?"

"It's not just about that though, right?"

"I don't know. If I never left my house again and I didn't already have you, I don't think being straight or gay would matter at all. Well, outside of my Google searches."

"Gross."

"Sorry."

"It's bigger than that," she said. "Maybe that's part of it. Of what's wrong with him. He doesn't know how to be himself because he thinks it doesn't matter who he is. This could factor hugely into his social anxiety."

"Lisa, you meet this guy *once* and the second you show up again, he's coming out to you. That doesn't sound like someone who isn't being himself, does it?"

"No," she answered. "That's what makes it more confusing. He's a little anxious, sure, but otherwise, he's like us. Easy to talk to. Funny. Really funny, actually. I just don't know why he can't deal with anything out here. I think he's as capable as anyone."

"Obviously not," Clark said. "But you think being his friend is the best way to help him?"

"That's the plan," she said. "Start with me and then eventually bring you into the mix. Show him what he's missing out here."

"Oh, is that right? I'm part of this now?"

"Only if you want to be. You said yourself that you're getting tired of the guys from the team."

"So tired," he said. "Everything is such a pissing contest with those morons."

"Well, there you go."

"You know, you could probably just make something up for your essay and still get that scholarship," he said.

"I know that. But, I want to help him. It's not just about the scholarship anymore."

"You promise?"

"I promise," she said. "Give me a few more weeks with him. I don't want to overwhelm him and since you'll probably dethrone me as his new best friend, I'd like to get to know him a little better."

"I *am* very fun," he said.

"Let me guess. Right now you are wearing pajama pants, probably nothing else, and there's a bag of Doritos somewhere visible in the room. Maybe even a doughnut or two."

"Amazing. How do you do it?"

"Magic," she said. "What's your sister doing?"

"Same thing. We've been playing video games for, like, five hours. I'm not proud, Lisa. But, also, I *am* proud?"

"It's funny," she said. "The second I start hanging with a dorky recluse, you turn into one. What is this *life*?"

The next day, Lisa was happy to find Ron's car in the driveway. She didn't like him much, but her mom did. And she was a lot happier when he was home. It sucked that they were the way they were: one of those couples that's either all over each other or at each other's throats. But some people are just wired that way, Lisa thought. And she was glad she wasn't one of them.

Around lunchtime, she was looking over some history notes when her phone rang. It was Solomon.

"Didn't I just talk to you a few hours ago?" she answered.

"What happened last night?"

"We watched the best movie ever and you came out to me."

"Yes, yes," he said. "Being out is exhausting. I just woke up like an hour ago."

"And what have you accomplished? Because me? I've already run two miles, written a book report, and started studying for a test."

"Yeah. I spent twenty minutes watching a documentary on eels until I got too creeped out to keep going."

"Okay . . . so, you're having a productive day, that's good."

He laughed harder than she'd expected. It was a great laugh—that kind where you can actually hear the *ha-ha-ha*'s if you listen closely enough.

"Yeah . . . umm . . . did you know the lifespan of an eel is about eighty-five years?"

"That's horrifying. Solomon, did you call to invite me over?"

"Maybe."

"Go ahead. Just do it. Don't be shy."

"Are you serious?" he asked.

"If you want to be friends, you're going to have to do the things that friends do. They call each other up and invite each other over. You're halfway there."

"Fine. Do you?"

"Do I what?"

"Do you want to come over today?"

"I'm actually pretty busy," she said, holding in a laugh.

"You've got to be kidding me."

"I am. How's two o'clock sound? I've got about thirty more pages of notes to look over."

"That's perfect," he said. "I mean, if you want to."

"Solomon," she scolded. "You were doing so well. What's this *if you want to* business? I want to, okay?"

"Great," he said. "What do you want to do?"

"Do you play chess?"

"I do. Very poorly."

"Awesome. So chess it is then. Do you have a set?"

"Yeah," he said. "It's an Adventure Time edition. Please don't make fun of me."

"Are you kidding? Clark and I watch it all the time."

"You're shitting me!" he said.

"Am not."

When she got to his house a couple of hours later, he had the chess set ready to go at the dining room table. She'd actually never spent any time in this room and it looked like nobody else had, either. Maybe this was an eat-on-your-own family like hers had always been. For whatever reason, she sort of hoped not, though.

"What's your favorite food?" she asked, taking a seat.

"Are we in kindergarten?"

She looked down at the chess set and back up at him with one arched eyebrow.

"Okay," he said, sitting down. "Pizza, probably."

"Ugh," she said. "So boring, Solomon."

"You can say Sol if you want," he said. "Or Solo."

"Can I be honest with you?"

"Yeah."

"I think *Solo* sounds kind of mean."

"Nah," he said. "Think *Han*, not *Lonely Agoraphobe*."

"Ah . . . yeah, that works."

"I like *Sol* though. My great-granddad was a Sol."

"Mine was *Gator*," she said.

"Wait . . . *Gator* Praytor?"

"Yep," she said, lowering her head in fake shame. "He was a zoologist. I'm not even kidding."

"What was his real name though?"

"Dick," she said.

"Well, see, that's just a man who made good choices."

"Okay, okay. Are you ready to be annihilated at chess?"

"Ready as I'll ever be," he said. "Who goes first?"

"Oh, Sol. You're not off to a great start."

"Shit," he said. "White first. I remember."

"You know, you've got quite the mouth for someone who's never been to high school."

"Don't let my folks fool you. When no one's around, they talk like sailors."

"My mom made me wash my mouth out with soap last year," she said. "I called my stepdad a *son-of-a-bitch*. Funny thing is, she was only mad about the cursing."

"I don't do it much around them," he said.

"That's just *your* form of rebellion. If they were criminals, you'd probably grow up to be a cop. The world is a mysterious place."

"Or maybe you just bring out my bad side," he said, moving his first pawn two spaces.

"I doubt that," she said, moving one of her knights.

She didn't care who won the game, really. She was trying something she'd read about online that morning. Game therapy. It was supposed to relax and distract a patient enough to help them open up more about personal or painful things. Now that Solomon had shown so much progress so quickly, she wanted to see how far she could push him without him realizing he was being pushed.

Lisa won the first game, trapping Solomon's king with a pawn and a rook. Then, without a word, she watched as he reset all the pieces on the game board and carefully turned it around so the white pieces were facing her.

"I'm better with black," he said.

Halfway through the game, it looked like Solomon might actually win. He was so focused on the board that he hadn't looked up in fifteen minutes. Maybe it was working, she thought. Maybe now was as good a time as ever for her to play therapist.

"So, aside from losing this game, what's your biggest fear?"

"Being buried alive," he answered with little pause.

"That's reasonable."

"Yours?"

"Tornados. Don't ask me why. I've never even been close to one."

"They're giant wind vortexes that destroy whole towns," he said. "Respect."

"And, I don't know . . . I guess being stuck in Upland forever, too."

"And *that* is where we differ," he said, moving a pawn. "Where do you want to go?"

"Anywhere," she said. "Somewhere bigger. A big city. The suburbs bore the hell out of me."

"But they're full of old people and little kids and crazy

guys like me," he said. "What's not to love?"

"Do you do that a lot?" she asked. "Call yourself *crazy*?"

"Only when it's funny or gets me out of chores."

"So, your biggest fear is being buried alive. Okay. What about something that could *actually* happen to you?"

"Like being asked repeatedly what my biggest fears are when I'm trying to beat you at chess?"

"Sorry," she said. "The mystery will have to stay a mystery I guess."

He looked up from the board and right into her eyes, like he was asking her what she thought she was doing without saying anything. She answered by looking down and capturing one of his bishops with her queen.

When the game was over, Lisa followed him back to his bedroom, where he dug through some boxes in his closet before finally pulling out a small stack of comic books.

"Here," he said. "Give these to Clark. I've read them a hundred times."

"For real?" she said, flipping through the one on top. "Thanks."

"No worries. My one stipulation is that he can't hide them. They must be displayed proudly in his home for all to see. It's the only way."

"I'll relay the message," she said. "Who knows, maybe you two can meet someday."

"Maybe," he said. "If you think he'd want to."

"You kidding? It's all he talks about. I think he's jealous."

"Jealous of the crazy gay kid. That doesn't sound right."

"Hey, Sol," she said, her tone getting serious for a second. "Those are two things about you out of a million. Don't box yourself in."

"Too late for that," he said, looking all around the room with an unconvincing smirk. "Much too late."

THIRTEEN
SOLOMON REED

Solomon's grandma always brought a gift. Always. She'd come over every other week or so and, without a word, hand Solomon a nicely wrapped box or a gift bag overflowing with tissue paper. Then she'd look on with big, excited eyes while he unwrapped it, always snapping a photo with her phone. He liked to imagine a big wall in her house that was covered with hundreds of these nearly identical pictures of him holding video games or DVDs and being forced to smile.

But when she came over on that Monday in April to celebrate his new social life, Grandma walked in with her hands full of pool toys instead. Bright-colored floating noodles flopped around in the air above her, bumping into the walls as she started showing off each gift to Solomon and his parents.

"For diving," she said excitedly, letting five yellow plastic rings slide down one arm and onto the floor. "Goggles. Even some floaties, you know, in case you forgot how to swim!"

Solomon stepped forward and started helping her—

finding more diving rings, three more pairs of goggles, some swim trunks, and even a Speedo. He held the bright orange bikini up and gave his grandmother a puzzled look.

"You never know," she said. "You could train for the Olympics with all the time you have."

Solomon took the Speedo and rubber band–style shot it at his dad, who caught it midair and then held it up to his waist.

"Oh yeah, I'm going to look *good* in this puppy."

"Grandma, cancel the pool," Solomon said.

"Fine," she said. "You all make fun, but in Europe, that's what they wear. A little culture wouldn't hurt anyone around here."

"Noted," said Solomon's dad, grabbing one of the pool noodles and hitting his son on top of the head with it.

"Thanks, Grandma," Solomon said, putting a pair of goggles on. "How do I look?"

"Perfect."

And since it looked like maybe she'd cry, he pretended he was swimming through the air toward her and gave her a quick hug.

Later, Solomon inflated a large bright green inner tube on the living room floor while his parents and grandma chatted over coffee and dessert on the sofa. When he was done, he stood up and fell backward right into the center of it.

"Looks comfortable," Grandma said. "Your father broke his tailbone in middle school and had to sit on something very similar. Only smaller, of course. You remember that, Jason?"

"I broke my ass, Mom. Of course I remember."

"I felt like the worst mother in the world," she said, laughing so hard tears were coming out of her eyes. "I lost it every time I saw that little cushion. I couldn't help it."

"You see, Sol?" his dad said. "This is why we never let you stay at Grandma's when you were younger."

"That's not true," she said. "I kept you all the time. You were my little sidekick."

"She used you to sell houses," his dad added. "Dressed you in a little suit and tie and took you with her to show properties."

"Resourcefulness is *not* something I'll apologize for," she defended. "That's how you build a business."

"Joan Reed Realty," Solomon's dad said. "We'll take you home . . . after you give us your life's savings."

"I miss grounding you," Grandma said, scowling at her son. "Sol, tell me all about this Lisa girl."

"She's nice," he said.

"Nice?" she asked, looking over toward her son and daughter-in-law. "This kid of yours, he's so . . . expressive, you know?"

"We've worked very hard on him," Solomon's dad joked.

"C'mon, spill it, kid," Grandma said.

"Okay, umm . . . she's funny, too. And, I don't know, *laid back*, I guess. It just wasn't as hard as I thought it would be."

"That's good to hear," she said, looking around to each person in the room and nodding her head.

"Yeah," he agreed. "She came over Saturday night, too."

"And yesterday," his dad added.

"Really?" Grandma asked. "Solomon, do you have a girlfriend?"

"No. It's not like that," he said.

"Okay, so what did you and your *friend* do then, with all that time together?"

"We watched movies and played chess mostly."

"Speaking of," Grandma said. "Let's you and me go play a game so I can get the real gossip, okay?"

"Sure."

Once they were in the den, he set up a little folding table and they both started shuffling without a word. Skip-Bo was no joke to Solomon and his grandmother and since he'd been on a winning streak lately, he knew she'd be out for blood. But as soon as the cards were dealt and they started playing, all she wanted to do was talk about Lisa.

"Wow," she said. "You're really doing it, aren't you?"

"What?"

"You've made a new friend. You say you're going in the backyard soon. You're getting better, kiddo."

"Please don't say that."

"Why not? Why shouldn't we celebrate it?"

"Because it's just too much, okay? It's not that big a deal."

"It's big enough," she said. "Who knows, in a few years, you could be ready to face the world again."

"Trust me," he said. "It's not a switch I can turn on and off, Grandma."

"Slow and steady wins the race," she said.

"I'm not sure that applies here."

"Even so," she said, "don't shut out the possibility of getting better, okay?"

"I'll try not to," he said.

When she went to leave that night, his grandma hugged

him a little tighter than usual and he knew why. She was proud of him. And that was something very new. He knew how to be pitied and misunderstood, but being admired wasn't in his wheelhouse quite yet. Though, it was certainly something he could get used to.

He got his schoolwork done super early the next day so he could relax a little bit before Lisa came over. He didn't really know what they were going to do, but he'd thought about teaching her to play Munchkin, which was this strategy card game his parents had bought him, but didn't really like playing. He couldn't even get past explaining the rules to his grandma before she said, "This sounds too hard for someone my age." It's funny how she only ever mentioned her age when she didn't feel like doing something.

But he knew Lisa would catch on quick, especially after seeing her play chess. He wanted a rematch but decided to challenge her to something she wasn't so familiar with first. You know, remind her whose house it was and all. This was *his* territory. *His* fortress of solitude, impenetrable to the outside world.

Only, that wasn't so true anymore, was it? Something new was here, in the form of this surprisingly familiar seventeen-year-old girl. And as soon as Solomon opened the front door that afternoon, Lisa walked in with a casualness outmatched only by his grandmother's the previous day. She gave him a wave and a smile and moseyed over to the living room to sit down on the sofa.

"Pool's coming along," she said, gesturing toward the sliding glass door and out into the backyard.

"I hope it's not a trap," he said, sitting down.

"Not a bad trap to be in," she said. "I'm sure your parents will use it either way."

"Sure they will," he said. "But I *am* going out there."

"Good," she said. "Can I come to all your wild pool parties?"

"Oh no," he said jokingly. "Co-ed fraternization is strictly prohibited."

"Well," she said, picking up the Speedo from the cushion beside her. "It looks like boys wearing Speedos isn't."

"My grandma. She bought out a sporting goods store or something."

"Your grandmother bought you a Speedo?"

"Yeah . . . I didn't try to defend it, okay?"

"Hey, I'm more than used to Speedos."

"I don't have a response for that," he said.

"Clark," she said. "Water polo."

"Oh, right. That can't be comfortable."

"He loves it," she said. "I think he's an exhibitionist."

"Feel free to provide photographic evidence at your leisure," he said, turning red.

"Solomon Reed! Did you just make a sexy joke about my boyfriend?"

"Maybe. How does water polo work again?"

"Okay . . . so, think hockey but in a pool with way less clothing."

"Awesome," he said. "Is he any good?"

"When he wants to be. He's got motivation issues. I was sort of hoping he'd try for a scholarship, but I can't really figure out what his plan is."

"There's plenty of time left, right?"

"Not really. Applications are due to most schools by December."

"That's terrifying."

"I can't wait," she said. "I fear I've outgrown my peers."

"I'm your peer," he said with a blank face.

"My *other* peers," she corrected.

"Even Clark?"

"Especially Clark."

"Oh," he said, following it with nothing because that's how much he knew about relationships.

"Sorry. I just wish he'd take things more seriously sometimes. Having a plan is sort of my thing."

"No surprises," he said. "You've clearly come to the right place."

"So far, you've been all surprises."

"Right. Well, I've reached my quota then."

"The Land of Solomon," she said. "Come for the holodeck, stay for the pasty kid in the Speedo."

"I'm *not* wearing that thing. And you do realize I spend ninety-eight percent of my time reading and watching TV alone, right?"

"I realize you *used* to," she said with confidence.

Lisa came over every day that week. She'd only stay two or three hours, just long enough to play a couple of games or watch a movie, and by the time the weekend rolled around, Solomon knew to expect her around three thirty or four every afternoon. And he could feel himself relaxing a little more with each visit.

On Saturday, Solomon's mom insisted on cooking them lunch. He knew it would happen eventually—a mostly silent meal where he'd be forced to look on in horror as his parents took turns interviewing her between bites of food. Up to that point, they'd pretty much stayed out of the way, so well that he suspected they were making sure she'd be sticking around before getting too attached.

"I hope you like enchiladas, Lisa," his mom said as they all sat down to eat.

"I do. The cheesier the better."

"These are vegan," Solomon said with a serious expression.

"Oh . . . well, vegan sounds great, too. Vegan all around."

"He's kidding," his dad said.

"But you've passed an important test," his mom added.

"Very important," Solomon echoed. "Always love whatever the cook cooks, isn't that right, Dad?"

"That's right. Unless it's tofurkey."

"I try it *one* time and now I'll never hear the end of it," his mom said. "Who wants to say grace?"

"Is it Christmas?" Solomon asked, looking at her like she'd offered to sacrifice a lamb on the dining room table.

"Do you say grace at your house?" she asked Lisa.

"Mom . . . seriously? The only two rules of a dinner party are no discussing religion or politics."

"Lisa, you a big fan of democracy?" his dad asked with a grin on his face.

"I'm an agnostic fiscal conservative, actually," Lisa said. "But I think you should make Sol say grace anyway."

"Fine," he said, bowing his head. "Thank you for the

world so sweet. Thank you for the food we eat. Thank you for the birds that sing. Thank you, God, for everything. Amen."

"Amen," his parents and Lisa said in unison.

"Also, praise Xenu," he added.

"Praise Xenu," they echoed.

"That was adorable," Lisa said.

The rest of the meal went better than Solomon had expected. They *did* interview her, but it was innocent enough, and by dessert, he just sat back and watched as they all shared stories and laughed at one another's little jokes. It was as familiar as when his grandma was over, but more exciting. She was new, after all, and as he watched his parents hanging on her every word, he thought maybe they'd needed a Lisa Praytor just as badly as he had.

Over the next three weeks and into May, Lisa spent most of her free time at the Reeds'. She'd stay for dinner most nights, helping Solomon set the table and do the dishes afterward, like they were siblings sharing chores. And he could quickly feel the rhythm in his house changing—the day would be quiet as ever and then Lisa would show up and they'd all fight over her attention. But, she seemed to love it, always down for an in-depth conversation about film history with Solomon's dad or a baking lesson with his mom.

"No one here cares about cake, Lisa. It's my living nightmare," Valerie Reed said to her one evening as they poured batter into a cupcake mold.

"I didn't peg you for a baker," Lisa told her. "I didn't think you'd have time, I guess."

"I used to make birthday cakes to help pay for college. My aunt had a cake shop. Taught me everything she knew. Plus, you can't do root canals at home. I get bored."

One day, Lisa and Solomon were putting together a puzzle that had been taking up one end of the dining room table for going on two weeks. They listened to the radio, silently scanning for the right pieces and bobbing their heads to the music. Having a friend was no longer new to him, but he was still Solomon—and that meant he'd sometimes overthink every little thing they said to each other, letting their conversations hang in the air around him for hours after she'd leave, hoping he hadn't said anything stupid or offensive or too immature. Before her, he had nothing to lose except the safety of his home. But now, since she was part of that, too, he couldn't risk losing her.

"You're telling me you've *never* chatted with anyone online?" Lisa asked.

"Do *Star Trek* forums count?"

"Sure," she said. "But you never Skype with anyone?"

"Strangers looking at me through my computer screen? No thanks."

"Agreed," she said. "You know . . . there are *sex* ones, too. Like video chat rooms."

"I know. What's wrong with people?"

"I'm not sure," she said. "But I put a little piece of tape over my webcam a long time ago. I don't trust any of my electronics anymore. My phone probably just sent our whole conversation to Wal-Mart or something."

"Yep. We'll get coupons in the mail for condoms and webcams tomorrow."

"America the beautiful," she said.

"Even on the forums, I don't post too much," he said. "It's just never really been my thing."

"I like that. A true loner."

"The world's too big," he said. "And the Internet is way too big. I don't hate everybody. I hope you don't think that. I just have to protect myself—and I can't deal with talking to a bunch of strangers who could be anybody from anywhere. It just never feels real."

"I get that."

"Lisa?"

"Yeah?"

"Don't you miss Clark?"

"Say what?" she asked, finally looking up at him.

"Well, you're over here, like, every day and, I don't know, I guess I'm starting to feel like I'm stealing you or something."

"Are you getting tired of me? Is that what this is?" she asked, trying to stop her widening smile.

"Shut up. I just . . . I think maybe I'm ready to meet him."

"Oh yeah?"

"I mean, it's been over a month now. The guy's going to hate me if I don't start sharing you a little."

"He has his video games," she said, slapping Solomon's words away in the air.

"I'm serious, though," he said. "You think he'll like me?"

"Why's it matter what I think?"

"He's your boyfriend," he said. "Maybe we won't get along."

"That would be unfortunate," she said. "However, impossible."

"You don't think the gay thing will bother him?"

"Bother him? Oh my God, he'll probably volunteer to drive you to a pride parade on day one."

"He can't be *that* good."

"I have this theory that he wears a Superman costume under his clothes at all times," she said.

"His name *is* Clark."

And then, like a sign from Jor-El of Krypton himself, Lisa's phone started lighting up and vibrating on the table.

"Speak of the devil," she said, picking it up. "Can you give me one second?"

"Sure."

"Lisa Praytor, Girlfriend of Your Dreams," she answered, shooting Solomon a big smile. "Uh-huh. Right. Well . . . okay. Can you do me a favor? Exactly. Thank you. Love you too. Okay. Bye."

"How's he doing?" Solomon asked, looking down at the puzzle.

"Super," she said. "I'll talk to him later, okay? About coming over."

"Now I'm nervous."

"Don't be. I'm jazzed about this, Sol. Do you believe in destiny?"

"Not really. But I like the idea of *you* believing in it."

"Then we're all set, aren't we? And you'll see."

"Lisa," he said, knowing she could hear his quickened breathing.

Solomon had never had a panic attack in front of her, but

there'd been a few close calls for sure—a couple of times he'd even pretended to go to the bathroom just so he could calm down and breathe like normal. He was sure she'd noticed, though, and just hadn't said anything. Maybe it made her uncomfortable. Or maybe she was like everyone else and just didn't know what to say or do. Most people would rather do nothing than risk doing the wrong thing—that's something Solomon learned a long time before shutting them all out.

"Okay . . . okay . . . ," she said calmly. "It's okay. You're good, Sol."

"Sorry," he said, leaning forward and resting his face in his hands.

"No apologies. Just breathe and count to ten, okay? That's good . . . now exhale slowly at five. You've got this, buddy."

He looked up at her, counting in his mind, and instead of hiding his face in embarrassment or leaving the room, he did exactly what she told him to do. It was five minutes of panic in an otherwise quiet, normal day—five minutes of near silence that told him more than any conversation they'd ever had. He was safe with her. She did something instead of nothing. And suddenly destiny didn't seem all that far-fetched an idea.

FOURTEEN
LISA PRAYTOR

The second Solomon mentioned Clark coming over, Lisa knew she'd earned his complete trust. It wasn't a far leap, of course, seeing as she'd practically become a member of his family. And what could've been an obligatory friendship with a disturbed boy had, in actuality, become one of the healthiest relationships in her life with one of the more levelheaded people she'd ever met. And, lest you forget, it was going to make all of her dreams come true.

It was finally time for Solomon to meet Clark and realize that no matter how well you hide, the world finds you and gives you reasons to come out of the shadows. Lisa had already saved him from complete solitude, so now it was time to give him another friend on the outside. She knew as soon as Clark walked in with that big sincere smile and those sea-green eyes that Solomon, gay or not, would be enamored. Clark was one of those guys whose club you want to be in. And it was something you could tell just by seeing him—a familiarity and kindness that made strangers approach him all the time to ask for directions or to see if he was someone they knew. It was a specific kind of effortless charm that Lisa couldn't quite understand, but had certainly fallen victim to. And she was banking on similar results with Solomon.

When she left Solomon's house later that night, she went straight to Clark's and the second he opened the door, she looked him in the eyes and said, "It's time."

"Time for what?" he asked blandly, letting her in and taking a seat on the couch.

"Solomon. You. Me."

"Oh. I didn't think that was ever going to happen." He looked straight ahead at the TV.

"Look, I know I've been gone a lot lately."

"A lot?" he said, turning her way. "If I didn't see you at school I wouldn't even remember what you look like."

"Like you'd ever forget that," she joked.

"Don't do that," he said. "I'm allowed to be frustrated, Lisa."

"I know. But, this will fix everything."

"You think so?" he said sarcastically. "I can't wait to be the third wheel with you and the kid you're scamming."

"Watch it," she said, shooting him a look that made him flinch.

"Seriously, though. Am I supposed to pretend you're not using him? Do I have to lie, too?"

"I'm not lying," she said. "I *am* his friend. That part's real. It didn't have to be, but it is. And he never has to find out anyway. We're the only ones who know about that essay."

"Shit. Tell me why I'd want to do this again?"

"Because he needs you," she said. "And I need you. I

know it feels wrong, I do. I'm not naive. But I think it's the only way. Plus, it's too late to undo what I've done . . . which is nothing short of damn impressive in terms of experimental psychological treatments."

"Jesus, Lisa. Talk like a human."

"Clark, you're going to meet him and you're going to know why I can't give up. You'll see what I see. We have to help him out of there. The world needs him."

"Fine," he said. "But if he's weird, I'm not going back. I don't care if it ruins your *experimental psychological treatment* or not."

Since Lisa was afraid Clark would change his mind again, she planned to take him over to Solomon's the very next day. It would work perfectly since Jason and Valerie were having one of their date nights. Lisa figured the fewer people the better, just in case Solomon, or Clark for that matter, was feeling particularly anxious.

When they were standing at his front door the next afternoon, Lisa looked over at Clark and just by raising one eyebrow, asked if he was ready.

"I feel like I should have a gift or something," he said.

"You're not taking him to prom. Just relax."

When the door opened, Solomon stood silently on the other side. He was wearing a pair of blue jeans, something Lisa had never seen on him, a button-down shirt, and, much to Lisa's surprise, shoes.

"New shoes?" she asked.

"Yeah," he said, looking down at them. "Mom had to guess my shoe size. They're a little big."

"Why do you need them?" Clark asked. "I mean,

sorry . . . just . . . I don't think I'd ever wear them if I . . ."

"Sol, meet Clark Robbins. Master of the foot-in-mouth."

"Hi," Solomon said.

"I've heard a lot about you, Solomon."

Clark extended a hand and Lisa watched as they shook, him standing outside, Solomon standing inside, the divide between their worlds never clearer to her. And, like it was just another day, Solomon stepped aside and closed the door after they'd entered.

"You guys want something to drink?" he asked. "A snack maybe? Mom said to ask as soon as you got here."

"No thanks," Lisa said. "And don't offer Clark food. He eats like a pre-hibernation bear."

"I do," he said. "It's disgusting."

"No food then," Solomon said. "Should we sit or something?"

Lisa led the way to the living room and took a seat on the sofa. She crossed her legs and looked up with a face that said, *You should be sitting down, too, you morons.* So, Solomon took the chair by the fireplace and Clark sat next to Lisa, throwing his arm over the back of the sofa.

"This is weird, yeah?" Solomon asked, looking at the floor.

"You know what's weird?" Clark said. "Stonehenge."

"And Easter Island," Lisa added.

Solomon looked up at them the way he should've—like they weren't making any sense—and then let out a little laugh.

"Well, Clark," he said, "as you can see, I don't get out much. So, please explain to me why water polo is fun."

"Water polo? I thought I was just on a really bad swim team."

Lisa rolled her eyes at Solomon, who was, of course, laughing with Clark. These two were a match made in bad joke heaven.

"I've been trying to get a laugh like that out of him for a long time," Lisa said, crossing her arms.

"Can I ask you guys something?" Solomon said, his expression suddenly grave.

"Sure."

"How do you do it? These things are killing me."

He raised one leg and pointed to his shoe. It looked about a size too big and was a little out of style. This made her like him even more.

"You're going to have to get used to them again," Lisa said. "Your feet have become too delicate."

"Virgin feet," Clark added without hesitation.

"Great band name," Solomon said.

"*Clark Robbins and the Virgin Feet*," Lisa said.

"I like it." Clark nodded. "Or maybe just *Virgin Foot*."

"Ew," Lisa said. "You made it weird."

"Did I?" he asked Solomon.

"Kind of."

"Okay . . . okay," Clark said. "Can I ask you something, dude?"

"Yeah," Solomon said, looking a little worried.

"You *never* leave the house? Like, not even a foot? In secret maybe?"

"Clark," Lisa snapped.

"Don't get me wrong," Clark continued. "You could do

worse. I mean . . . if you have to be inside all the time, at least your house is nice. But, don't you ever want to go out there?"

"Well, yeah," Solomon said, looking toward Lisa. "Does he not know about the pool?"

He pointed toward the glass door to their left and out to the large hole in the yard.

"You think I'm just here to play chess?" Clark said. "I was promised pool parties and babes in bikinis and *Star Trek* marathons."

"You were promised maybe one and a half of those things," Lisa corrected.

"Fair enough. It's going to be awesome, man. It's our only real defense against global warming."

"Swimming?" Solomon asked.

"You get in a pool and tell me the world's on fire. I don't think so."

"That doesn't make any sense," Solomon said.

"Oh yeah," Lisa said. "Clark doesn't believe in global warming. It's the only thing he thinks his mom's right about."

"Well, she also thinks I'm smart. Which I can't argue with."

"He doesn't always try to be this funny," Lisa said. "This is Nervous Clark. A string of one-liners."

"Guilty," Clark said.

"Why would *you* be nervous?" Solomon asked.

"Meeting new people, you know," Clark said.

"Tell him what else," Lisa urged.

"Oh yeah," Clark said. "I hope this isn't rude and I know

we just got here and all, but I hear word of a holodeck and I need that dream to come true whenever you're ready."

"Okay, umm . . . sure, we can go see it if you want," Solomon said, standing up.

"Maybe I should sit this one out," Lisa joked.

"Never," Clark said.

Lisa had a hard time buying Clark's excitement as they followed Solomon through the kitchen and to the garage door. And she thought it looked like Solomon was just as excited as he was. When he'd shown *her*, he was almost embarrassed.

They stepped inside and Clark tightened his grasp on Lisa's hand before letting it go. He stood in the center of the room and slowly turned all the way around, looking at the floor, walls, and ceiling with this awestruck expression on his face. Solomon had that same look, but not because of the room. He stared right at Clark until he caught Lisa's eye and snapped out of it. When he closed the door, the room was pitch-black, except for the tape.

"Incredible," Clark said in a whisper, like he'd be saying it to himself even if no one else were around.

"It's kind of ridiculous, I guess," Solomon said.

"Not at all," Clark argued. "Not even a little."

Lisa stood close enough to Clark to see him close his eyes for a second and then open them back up.

"Okay, quick," he said. "If you could be any character on *The Next Generation* who would you be?"

"Easy," Solomon said. "Data. For sure."

"That makes sense," Clark said.

"You?"

"I always liked Wesley Crusher."

"What?" Solomon was appalled. "Nobody likes Wesley Crusher."

"Why not?" Lisa asked.

"Because he's a total Mary Sue," Solomon said. "He's too perfect."

"But he's always saving the day," Clark argued. "Like, always."

"Exactly. He's just a talking deus ex machina. Everybody on the ship treats him like a dumb kid, then he saves them at the last minute and, every single time, they go right back to treating him like a dumb kid again. Do I need to remind you that the starship *Enterprise* is full of genius scientists and engineers? Why's this kid who can't get into Starfleet Academy smarter than all of them?"

"Good point," Clark said. "He's still my choice, though. So, umm . . . where's the ON switch to this room?"

"I know, right?" Solomon said. "It's just paint and tape."

"You watch *Community*?" Clark asked.

"I've seen an episode or two."

"One of the characters has a room like this. Calls it the Dreamatorium. But his works, sort of. I'll show you sometime."

"That would be awesome," Solomon said. "Why can't it be real? Where's the future we were promised, man?"

"For real," Clark said. "We're supposed to have cooler things than drones that deliver toilet paper."

"Drones deliver your toilet paper?" Solomon asked.

"Okay, so that *is* kind of cool. But, still. Where's my virtual reality? Where's my hover car? And where the *hell* is teleportation?"

"Why don't we teleport back to the living room, guys?" Lisa suggested. "I'm sorry to tell you that this room sort of gives me a headache."

"Fine," Clark said, disappointed. "But can I ask you one more thing?"

"Sure," Solomon said.

"Do you ever stand in here with that garage door open?"

"No I do not."

"Interesting," Clark said.

When they were back in the living room, seated exactly how they'd been before, the awkward silence set in. It was inevitable, Lisa figured, but she was determined not to let any moment of this day be soured, so she immediately hopped up, walked over to the cabinet where they kept the board games, and opened it wide, turning to look their way.

"Let's teach Clark how to play Munchkin so we can destroy him."

"I'm in," Clark said.

"She's very good," Solomon added, standing up. "It's disturbing, actually."

"No mercy," Lisa said.

When they were all set up at the dining room table, Lisa knew she'd made the right decision. Already, Solomon seemed more relaxed as he shuffled the cards and started explaining the rules. She did notice a difference, though, between the way he'd taught her and the way he was teaching Clark. The first time, he'd haphazardly given her the basics of the game and, ultimately, decided to just start playing and teach her as they went along. But with Clark, he was taking the time to go over every little rule and circumstance possible. And even though it stretched out longer than it should have, Lisa knew why. He finally had something to say to Clark and he didn't want it to end.

FIFTEEN
SOLOMON REED

Solomon couldn't believe this guy. He knew five phrases in Klingon *and* Dothraki. And he showed off these skills with a confidence that normally would've annoyed Solomon. But, from Clark, it was endearing and innocent. It felt like he'd always been around. And just after Lisa beat them both at the first game, Solomon realized they'd been practically ignoring her the entire time.

"Sorry," he said, looking her way. "I bet we're boring you to death."

"I'm past death," she said, smiling. "Hell was great. Less *Star Trek* references."

They ended up playing two more rounds, with a break for pizza in between. Lisa won the first and Clark won the second. It was weird, having friends like this, at his house, playing a game like it was no big deal. It wasn't to them, he thought. Which was so perfect—nothing was forced. They were just there to have fun.

Mostly, though, he watched Clark. Every single turn he would silently inspect his hand, looking back and forth from the table to his cards before making a move. When he drew a good card, he'd raise his right eyebrow just slightly enough to be noticed and when he drew a bad card, he'd frown a little. And even despite noticing these things, Solomon was still too distracted to beat him.

"Beginner's luck," he said after the second game. "Your time will come. Rest assured."

"Oh yeah?" Clark asked. "You care to make it interesting?"

"I do," he replied. "I wager the hand of your lady."

"Wait . . . what?" Lisa said, helping put away the cards.

"Oh, you can have her," Clark joked. "What else you got?"

"Very funny," Lisa said. "It's getting kind of late."

"Yeah," Clark agreed. "Where are your parents?"

"They went to dinner and a movie," he said.

"Now *that* is something I bet you miss," Clark said. "Going to the movies, I mean."

"I do. But, I have Wi-Fi and TV, so it's not a big deal."

"But the *pop*corn," Clark added.

"Sometimes they bring some home."

"Dude, we could bring you stuff from the outside, too, you know."

"He's not in prison, Clark."

"Sorry . . . I didn't mean it like that."

"No, it's cool," Solomon said. "I don't miss much. It's easier than you guys think it is."

"I saw this movie called *Copycat* once," Clark said out of nowhere.

"I know that movie," Lisa interrupted. "With the chick from *Alien*."

"Yeah. Sigourney Weaver. Anyway, she played this criminal psychologist who couldn't leave her apartment.

But then she gets all wrapped up in helping this detective find a serial killer."

"Oh no. Do you guys need help finding a serial killer, too?" Solomon asked. "This explains everything."

"Or maybe someone *else* needed your help finding *us*," Clark said.

"That makes sense," Solomon said. "Now you're going to kill me?"

"*Serial* kill you," Clark said.

"Now you're just being ridiculous, dude."

"Why does, like, every show on TV have a serial killer now?" Lisa asked. "There are five in the world and a thousand on TV. Every week, it's a new sociopath making sculptures with human body parts."

"You have such a way with words, Lisa," Clark said.

"She's right, though," Solomon added. "If there were *that* many serial killers in real life, we'd all be scared shitless."

"Have you ever been scared shitless, though?" Clark asked. "Like, so scared that you can't even think about ever taking a shit again. You're just done. For life."

"You're so gross," Lisa said.

"Have you?" Solomon asked Clark.

"Oh yeah. This one time . . . I guess it was about a year ago . . . my friend TJ and I went in this doll room at his grandma's house and I swear to you we saw one move."

"A doll?" Solomon asked.

"Yeah. So, this room was filled floor to ceiling with those old creepy porcelain dolls. The ones with the evil eyes, you know, that follow you no matter where you go. She collected them. Must've been a real psycho because right when I stepped into that room, I felt the devil trying to get inside me."

"I don't believe in the devil," Solomon said.

"Me neither," Lisa added.

"You haven't seen what I've seen," Clark said with true terror in his eyes.

"He was really freaked out for a while," Lisa said. "It was hilarious."

"I still can't walk through the toy aisle at Target," he said.

"All right, I'm falling asleep," Lisa said, stretching her arms out above her head. "Thanks for letting us hang out, Sol."

"Yeah, anytime," he said.

He smiled and reached his fist out to meet hers. This is how they always said good-bye, but he got suddenly nervous about doing it in front of her boyfriend. When their knuckles met, Clark set one hand on top of theirs and shouted *One, two, three, break!*

"Weirdo," Lisa said. "Say good-bye, Clark."

"Well, the night was too short, my friend," Clark said, extending a hand to Solomon.

"What are you guys doing tomorrow?" he asked just as his hand gripped Clark's.

"Oh, umm. . . ." Clark had a surprised look on his face.

"Sorry," Solomon said. "I mean. Thanks for coming."

"I'm free tomorrow," Lisa said, looking Clark's way with wide eyes.

"Oh, yeah. Me too. It's Saturday, though, so I'm sleeping like half the day but that's it."

"Perfect," Lisa said. "I'll call when we're on our way."

After they were gone, Solomon walked to his room and fell back onto the bed, letting his feet dangle off one side. It was pitch-black except for a faint red glow from his alarm clock. It was so quiet suddenly, like it had always been. And even though he was a little relieved to finally be alone, he replayed the entire night in his head. He'd made it through without any problems. But instead of celebrating it, Solomon felt his heart racing and his breathing picking up and his hands shaking. He turned and grabbed a pillow, pressing his face into it and trying to take deep breaths. And there in the darkness he rode it out as he heard his parents getting home. When the door slowly opened a few minutes later, he pretended to be asleep, his face still covered.

The next afternoon, Lisa and Clark came over around three and as soon as Solomon answered the door, they each held out gifts for him.

"I thought I wasn't in prison," he said, blushing but trying to move past it.

"Well, these are really for all of us," Lisa said, holding up a plate covered in pink plastic wrap. It's a secret recipe. Best brownies you'll ever taste."

"It's the truth," Clark said. "And I brought some DVDs that are probably scratched up."

"Awesome. On all accounts. Come on in."

"Dude, are your parents ever home?" Clark asked, looking around.

"All the time," he answered. "They should be pulling up any minute, actually."

It didn't take long before Solomon challenged them to a rematch at Munchkin. It was already set up and everything. He'd been such a nervous wreck all day waiting for them—pacing around the house and watching the clock—that he started planning out everything they'd do that afternoon. Games were first, of course, but then he thought maybe they'd watch a movie or something. Sure, that was something he could do alone, but ever since Lisa showed up, he'd come to appreciate seeing how she reacted to things—what made her laugh or cringe or get sad. After a movie, he was hoping they'd stay late enough to watch *Saturday Night Live* with him. His parents had given up on the show years before, but it was a weekly tradition that Solomon refused to let go of and he was determined to share it with someone.

After their game, they all went to the kitchen to eat some leftover pizza from the night before. Solomon hoisted himself up onto the counter and Clark followed. Lisa sat on a swiveling bar stool and spun around slowly as they all talked and ate. And, for whatever reason, Clark decided to bring up dating—a topic Solomon wasn't too sure he was ready for.

"Okay . . . okay . . . but, like, don't you want to go on dates and stuff?" Clark asked.

Lisa suddenly stopped spinning and looked Solomon right in the eyes.

"I don't know," he answered, caught a little off guard.

"You don't know?" Clark asked. "Look, there are lots of dudes out there, Sol. *Lots* of dudes."

"Yeah, but, I'm here. They're there. It's just how it is."

"Clark, leave it alone," Lisa said.

"All right. Sorry. Just, you're a catch, man. Handsome. Funny. You've got *all seven seasons* of *STTNG* on DVD."

That made Solomon laugh and the red went out of his cheeks soon enough. This guy didn't care if he was gay or straight or agoraphobic or anything. He was perfect. And he was probably the closest Solomon was ever going to get to a boyfriend. Which, despite sounding heartbreaking, actually felt like a real win for a kid who'd only been slightly out of the closet for a month.

A few minutes later, Solomon's parents got home and walked in on the three of them joking around and eating in the kitchen.

"Troublemakers," Solomon's dad said.

"Mom, Dad, this is Clark."

Clark hopped down from the counter and walked over to shake their hands.

"Jason Reed. Nice to meet you," Solomon's dad said. "This is Valerie."

"Hi. So nice to meet you," Clark said.

"You have beautiful teeth," Valerie said. "Do you floss?"

"Every day," he answered. "And I've never had a cavity."

"Good to hear," she said. "Lisa, he's a keeper."

"I see you guys are getting a pool," Clark said. "What's that, a standard eight footer?"

"You looking to buy one yourself, Clark?" Jason asked with a grin.

"I wish," he answered. "I've been begging my mom for one since I was five."

"Come use ours anytime," Valerie said.

"Awesome."

"Yeah, even if you don't like Solomon," Jason joked.

"Wow. Nice, Dad. You guys want to go watch a movie or something?"

"Sure," Lisa said.

"Oh, I forgot to tell you," Clark said. "I brought *Community* so you could see the Dreamatorium."

"Awesome," Solomon said.

"Okay, you guys have fun with whatever all that means," Valerie said. "I've got a Pat Conroy book that isn't going to read itself."

"And I've got a lawn to mow," Jason said, walking away in the opposite direction of his wife.

"Dude, they're awesome."

"Yeah, I like 'em okay," Solomon said.

"No, really. My mom's a basket case, man. You've got it good."

"He's right," Lisa said. "You may suck at cards, but you definitely win the parent game."

"It's too bad I've driven them so crazy," he said. "They used to have fun. Used to go on trips and stuff. Last night was the longest they've been out in a while, aside from work."

"They afraid to leave you alone?" Clark asked. "You seem pretty self-sufficient to me."

"It's not that," he said. "It makes them feel guilty or something. I don't know. It's like they're holding out until I'm better."

"They don't make you see a shrink?"

"Used to," Solomon said. "Came here once a week."

"When did that stop?" Lisa asked.

"A little after the first year. She kept putting me on medicine that made me sick. I begged and begged and they finally told her to stop coming."

"I saw a therapist when I was younger," Clark said. "I was scared to sleep in my room alone."

"That's normal, though," Lisa said.

"Not when you're twelve," he added.

"I asked my dad if I could try marijuana once," Solomon blurted out.

"Seriously? Dude, we go to high school in California. We can get you weed."

"Noted," Solomon said. "So *that's* why they call it *high* school?"

"Boo," Lisa said. "Try again."

"Okay . . . okay . . . umm . . . *Upland*? More like *Highland*!"

Clark laughed, but Lisa just shook her head and tried not to smile. Solomon loved how she was always pretending like her sense of humor was above theirs when it was so clear to him that she loved every second of their stupid banter.

At around two in the morning, after more games, an especially lame episode of *SNL*, and way too many bad jokes, Lisa finally stood up and said it was time to go. Clark seemed as bummed as Solomon, but they all had that middle-of-the-night sleepy look in their eyes. Solomon walked them to the door and they said their good nights. He wanted to ask when he'd see them next, but he got shy about it at the last minute and didn't say anything.

He couldn't just invite them over every day and expect them to never say *no*.

Lisa hugged him around the neck before she stepped outside and as he went to give Clark a handshake, he was met with a big squeeze around the shoulders. He didn't know what to do or whether or not he should hug him back, so he just stood there with his arms limp and let it happen. Then Clark pulled away and had this huge smile on his face. "You're all right, man," he said.

Solomon watched them from the door as they walked down the driveway and got into Lisa's car. He waited as the engine turned on and the headlights lit up, giving them a wave as they backed out and drove off, his hand staying up in the air until they were out of sight. It hadn't happened before, really, so he tried to think about something else to keep from freaking out. But it wouldn't go away. He felt it. It was small and it was complicated, but he felt it all the same. He wanted to follow them. He wanted to walk outside and follow them into the world.

SIXTEEN

LISA PRAYTOR

It had been a very important weekend so far and despite being dangerously sleepy, Lisa drove Clark home with a rush of energy and excitement pumping through her veins. She knew he was on board now, especially after seeing the way he'd hit it off with Solomon. Lisa was overwhelmed with the feeling that she'd done something great by introducing the two of them. Now they'd have each other to talk holodecks and spaceships and she'd have her ticket out of Upland. Everybody would win.

"Thank you," she said to Clark when they got to his dad's.

"For what?"

"For this weekend. For not being too pissed at me to meet him."

"I'm still a little pissed," he said, smiling. "But I had fun. It's so . . . easy with him. Like I've known him forever. I think maybe I've been needing a Solomon Reed in my life."

"Is that right?"

"He's way better than my other options."

"I've met them, yes," she said. "TJ was asking about you at school yesterday. He made some stupid joke about you being a ghost."

"Good," he said. "I don't have anything to say to those guys anymore."

"Why's that?"

"Because they're jerks. Seriously, if they aren't making fun of someone then they're talking about whose girlfriend they want to bang."

"Gross."

"Yeah it is. And, look, I laugh sometimes. But then I feel like shit all day afterward. I'm not like them. And I don't want to be."

"I don't want you to be, either," she said.

"Well, while you've been hanging out with the coolest crazy person in history, I've been pretty much sitting around the house doing nothing. I know this is a big deal to you, but you can't just disappear. What if I don't get into a school near you, huh? You want to spend our last year together hanging out with someone else?"

"Look, I'm sorry. But, now you can come with me. See? It works this way."

"So, it's share you or be alone?" he asked, complete amazement in his eyes.

"No. That's not what I meant. Just, forgive me, okay? I'll do better. I will."

"Fine. You know Janis is pissed at you, too, right?"

"I have several unanswered texts that would indicate so."

"You should go see her," Clark suggested. "I know she's ridiculous, but you've been friends your whole lives."

"I haven't even told her about Sol. Like, not a thing."

"Well, there's only one way to fix that. I'm sure she'll understand."

"She'll want a boon," she said. "Justice is very important to her."

"Me too," he said, leaning over and kissing her forehead. "I'll see you tomorrow, Dr. Praytor."

The next day, Lisa woke up to a fight in the kitchen between her mother and Ron. This one was a doozy—slamming cabinets, yelling, a threat or two. She stayed in her room until it was over. But even then, she took her time going down the stairs, hoping to go undetected.

"Lisa?"

"Damn," she said to herself, rounding the corner into the kitchen. "Yeah?"

Her mom was sitting at the table in a silk robe and house slippers stirring a cup of coffee. This wasn't going to be pleasant, Lisa knew, but she had to do it. She couldn't just leave her mom alone like this, not after the fight she'd just heard.

"Are you okay?" she asked, sitting down across from her.

"Been better."

"I don't really know what to say, Mom."

"I know, sweetie. Me neither."

"Did he leave?" Lisa asked, reaching for her mom's cup of coffee and taking a sip.

"Yep."

She started crying, holding her chin to her chest, but not moving a muscle. Just quiet little whimpers that made

Lisa so angry. Why did she do this to herself? Why keep marrying the same man over and over again? Lisa didn't know how she could still be so surprised. Ron was a carbon copy of the one before him. And Lisa was pretty sure they were both just less charming versions of her dad. Sometimes she wondered if maybe she was crying over him, after all these years—if every new guy was just a poor replacement for the first one who left her.

Lisa reached a hand over and placed it on top of her mom's. She held it there, her thumb gripping her mother's fingers tightly, and then let go.

"Let me tell you about Solomon," she said, standing up to pour herself some coffee.

"Who?"

Lisa explained the whole situation to her mother, trying to distract her the only way she knew how—with something that closely resembled gossip. Her mom had wondered why she'd insisted on switching dentists, so this cleared some things up. Lisa, of course, left out the part about the scholarship essay. She couldn't risk being talked out of it, not after everything had been falling into place so well. And now with Clark on her team, she felt like getting Solomon out of that house was inevitable.

"Wait, wait," her mom interrupted. "You *and* Clark are hanging out with this kid?"

"Yes. He needs us, believe me."

"What kind of parents let their child act that way? Never leaving the house? Not going to school? Sounds like he needs a beating to me."

"Wow, Mom."

"No one wants to go to school, Lisa. Most kids would stay home all day if you let them. That's why you *don't* let them."

"I told you, he has a legitimate mental illness, Mom. Be more sensitive, please."

"They say that about alcoholics, too. They have a *disease.* Yeah right. The rest of us are supposed to feel sorry for all the drunks? Gimme a break."

"You should write for *Psychology Today* or something. Very inspiring stuff."

"Sorry. Well, good for you. And Clark. Just don't get into any trouble."

"Trouble? I don't even think that's possible with Solomon."

"I didn't think it was possible with three different husbands, but look where I am now."

"With an intelligent, beautiful daughter and a stable job?"

"Funny," she said. "You know what I mean."

"Mom," Lisa began, wanting so badly to just be honest, to tell her she had to stop looking for her happiness with these deadbeats. But she couldn't do it. "I love you."

"I love you, sweetie. Want me to make you some lunch?"

"No thanks. I've got to go talk to Janis. I've been neglecting her for weeks and I'm pretty sure she's pissed at me."

Janis Plutko worked in the Montclair Plaza Mall at a kiosk that sold perfume and Fossil watches. Before Solomon, Lisa would stop by several times a week and they'd eat cookies from the Great American Cookie Company in the food court and watch YouTube videos on their phones. On the rare occasion that Janis had a customer, Lisa would inundate them with free samples and usually end up talking them into at least buying something from the clearance rack. Janis always had her best sales days when Lisa showed up.

"Hey, you," Lisa said when she walked up to the kiosk. Janis turned her way and gave a sort of half smile.

"Look, I know you're pissed. Just let me take you to lunch so we can talk it out."

"What's to talk out?" she asked. "Some people just grow apart."

"Oh my God, really?"

"Lisa, I've barely seen you for a month. Do *not* treat me like I'm being irrational."

"Sorry. Just come to lunch with me. Can you take a break?"

She grabbed her keys off the counter by the register. "I've only got fifteen minutes."

They sat in the fairly crowded food court and shared some fries and a milk shake. Lisa couldn't get much out of Janis, but she tried her best. They'd been fighting on and off about stupid things since the fifth grade but she seemed really upset about this one, and Lisa knew she'd have to come clean about Solomon to be forgiven.

"Can you keep a secret?"

"Maybe," she whispered, leaning forward over the table.

"I've been working on a project. For college."

"What kind of project? Your cousin? Did you talk to him?"

"No. Do you remember the fountain kid?"

"Of course."

"I found him. He hasn't left the house in three years. I've been hanging out with him for weeks. He's going to get me that scholarship, Janis."

"Are you being serious right now?" she was still whispering, but it was getting louder with every word. "You *found* him? Are you insane?"

"No," Lisa said calmly. "I'm going to save his life."

Janis leaned back in her seat and shook her head for a few seconds with her eyes fixed on Lisa.

"Anyway, I'm really sorry I've been so flaky lately. But, I've made a lot of progress with Solomon. I think I could really be on to something here. With the right combination of game therapy and long-term social exposure, I could have him ready to face the world again by this fall."

"Lisa . . . you're pretending to be this boy's friend so you can write about it and get a scholarship."

"I'd hardly call him a boy. He's just a year younger than we are."

"Do you not understand why this is wrong? Because you're the smartest person I know and if you can't see this then I need to reevaluate a lot of things in my life."

"I get it," Lisa said. "But just like I told Clark—it's a means to an end. It's effective. If something works, if it cures him, then why does it matter *how* it works. He will never know *and* he'll be better. At this point, finding out is the only thing that could hurt him."

"And I guess you made it that way on purpose?"

"God, you act like I'm a con artist. I want to help him.

I've wanted to for a long time. You remember. Now I get to help him *and* go somewhere to learn how to help more people. What's wrong with that, Janis?"

"Let me meet him."

"No way," Lisa said.

"Why not?"

"He's not ready. He's still getting used to me. And he just met Clark. I can't overwhelm him."

"He's hanging out with Clark, too? Geez, Lisa, what kind of therapy is this?"

"Like I said. It's experimental. He just needs to learn that he doesn't have anything to be afraid of out here."

"Maybe he should be afraid. Did you consider that?"

"No," Lisa said, staring at her blankly.

"So I'm supposed to just forgive you for completely vanishing on me because it was all to help some crazy kid?"

"He isn't crazy," she snapped. "He just has a bad relationship with the world."

"He hasn't left his house in three years. That sounds crazy to me."

"He has acute agoraphobia brought on by severe panic disorder. When he leaves his house, his panic gets worse. Any one of us would do whatever we could to feel safe, just like he's doing. It's survival. But, that's no way to live and no matter what he says, I know he'll be happy out here. And we deserve him."

"Fine. Whatever. I forgive you, okay? But I don't approve."

"You don't have to. Just don't tell anyone. It could ruin everything."

"Fine. But I need a favor."

"Shit," Lisa said. "Don't say it."

"Camp Elizabeth. They need one more junior counselor and I know you had fun last summer no matter how much you try to pretend you didn't."

"Oh God. I can't, Janis. I purposefully kept my whole summer free to try and help Solomon and I . . ."

"Lisa," she said, crossing her arms. "You owe me. Come with me to camp and I'll forget you abandoned me like a dog."

"Okay . . . chill out a little."

"A *dog*, Lisa. A diseased dog. Left to fend for myself in the wilds of Upland High School. It's only two weeks. Starts June fifteenth. Say yes."

"Fine. I'll make it work. But I'm not teaching canoe."

"They need you to help teach canoe."

"Damn it."

Later that day, after Lisa had finished all her homework, she called Clark to see if she could come over. She figured a whole weekend hanging out with a stranger had earned him a little one-on-one time. Plus, she couldn't remember the last time they'd even made out.

"We should go see Sol," he said.

"Again?"

"Yeah, why not? I'm pretty sure he's not busy."

"I'm totally down," she said. "Unless you'd rather . . . umm . . . do something else, if you know what I'm saying?"

"Nah, I think we should see Sol. Maybe later?"

A little thrown off, but happy to continue with Solomon's treatment, Lisa called to see if he was game for visitors and, judging from his tone, he'd probably been waiting by the phone all day. She couldn't imagine what it had been like for him—to go so long without anyone but his parents or his grandma to talk to. And even though she felt like she'd made a lot of progress over the last month, it seemed like Clark had brought out something new in him . . . something less self-conscious and more confident. Maybe he was trying to impress him. Or, maybe Solomon just thought he and Clark lived in the same world, with the rest of us drifting in and out and never really understanding things like the intricacies of Klingon-Human relations or what the hell a khaleesi is.

When they got to Solomon's house, the Angels game was on and the whole family was watching it in the living room. They all watched the last three innings together and Solomon's mom would occasionally shout at the TV, which made Clark laugh every single time.

"She's very passionate about sports," Solomon said.

"And Sol's very passionate about making fun of his mom," Valerie added. "We almost had another kid in the hopes that we'd get a sports fan."

"You can adopt me," Clark said. "My mom hates sports and my dad didn't even teach me to throw a football."

"That's . . . well, that's just sad, son," Solomon's dad said, looking at Clark and shaking his head.

"Don't fall for that," Lisa said. "He's got like twenty older brothers. But they all moved away."

"It's really three, but it may as well be twenty," Clark added.

"Holy crap," Solomon said. "That's a lot of dudes."

"Are they all in college?" Solomon's mom asked.

"Two of them are," Clark answered. "And one's a tattoo artist in Hollywood."

"I always wanted a tattoo," Solomon said.

"Oh yeah? What would you get?" Lisa asked.

"The starship *Enterprise*."

"Yes," Clark said. "I bet my brother could come to you."

"Nope," Solomon's dad said. "Not till you're eighteen."

"What's it matter?" Solomon asked.

Jason just looked at him and, without a word of protest, Solomon dropped it and moved on. Lisa was simultaneously appalled and in awe of his restraint. Or maybe some families just don't fight. She'd probably never know, but she couldn't imagine these people ever raising their voices over anything more than a foul ball.

That Sunday night was the first of many nights like it. Lisa and Clark quickly became fixtures in the Reed home, showing up after school and staying for hours, sometimes into the early morning, even on school nights. With each new visit, Clark and Solomon would discover some shared interest—whether it was a B-movie Lisa had never heard of or some fan site she wouldn't be caught dead on. There always seemed to be something bringing the two of them closer together, and even though she wished it could just be her and Clark sometimes, she knew the sacrifice was worth it.

Plus, all that time as the third wheel had allowed her to very closely observe Solomon, probably much closer than she could have without Clark. She became a master at reading his mood, and she was always ready to step in and help in case the anxiety kicked in. His tells were subtle, but by that point, she knew them well. If something or someone was too loud or noisy, his left eye would twitch a little. This would also happen if he felt particularly unnerved or worked up about something he'd said or done. It was like he was reacting to actual physical pain sometimes. But most of the time, that's all it was—just a little twitch in one eye and then it was over.

She only worried when he left the room. No one needed to use the bathroom that often, and Lisa was betting, every time, that this was his way of catching his breath or grounding himself enough to avoid letting the anxiety take over. It would've been easy to forget sometimes that he was like that. Clark seemed to put it out of his mind completely. Which was good, Lisa thought. He treated Solomon just the way she'd hoped—like he was normal. And maybe that was part of getting him better. Maybe if someone like Clark could ignore Solomon's problems, then other people out there could, too.

But then, of course, Solomon had a full-blown meltdown in front of Clark. It was as surprising as it was quick. The three of them were sitting around the computer when he suddenly put his head down on the desk and started tapping his fingers quickly on the keyboard. Clark looked over at Lisa and shrugged, backing away and eyeing her like she should know what the hell they were supposed to do. She did. This would only be her second time witnessing one, but she sprung into action without hesitation. She took a deep breath, bent down so her face was right next to Solomon's, and she started to talk in the calmest tone possible.

"Sol, can you take some deep breaths with me?"

"Yes," he said. It sounded like he was crying, but she wasn't sure.

"Okay. I'm going to count to ten. Inhale slowly till five then exhale slowly."

So she counted and he breathed. Then she counted again. And Clark, not knowing what to say or do, took his phone out and stared at it, pretending that something was on the screen.

"Can you guys give me a minute?" Solomon asked, sitting back up but with his eyes closed.

She stood up and grabbed Clark's hand, leading him out into the hallway. With the door shut behind her, she put her arms around Clark's torso and squeezed tightly.

"Is he okay?" he whispered.

"I think so. Embarrassed, maybe."

"What should I say?"

"Just pretend it didn't happen unless he brings it up."

When Solomon opened the door, he looked a little better. Lisa could tell he'd wiped away a few tears, but he didn't look especially sad or ashamed or anything. Maybe a bit tired, but with as little sunlight as he got, he always kind of looked that way. He told them to come back in and then sat down at his desk again.

"Sorry," he said in a defeated tone.

"For what?" Clark asked.

"You don't have to do that," he said. "It actually helps me to not ignore it. It's weird."

"Are you okay?" Lisa asked.

"I'm fine. It was a fast one."

"How often does it happen?" Clark asked.

"Depends. That was the first one in a couple weeks."

"Damn," Clark said.

"It's okay, though," Solomon added. "I can handle that. Before, it was every day. Every day. At school. On the bus. In fountains from time to time."

"I never asked you," Lisa said. "Why the fountain?"

"It's the water," he said. "Calms me down."

"Is that why you want a pool?" Clark asked.

"That's some of it, I guess. I also just miss it. I miss going out there."

"I would too," Clark said. "So, you've got *two* good reasons to make it work."

"What if I can't, though?" he asked. "What if they go to all this trouble and have their hopes built up, and I can't take one step out there?"

"They'll be disappointed," Lisa said. "But they'll understand. Do you think they're betting on this being a sure thing?"

"Probably not."

"Then wait and see what happens before you accept defeat," Clark said. "Either way, you'll be okay. And, when the time comes, if you need us to help you, we will."

"You just want to swim in my pool," Solomon said with a big smile.

"You bet I do, whether you're out there or not, buddy," Clark said. "I was thinking of volunteering to be the pool boy. Build myself a little shack in the backyard maybe."

"Sol, if you don't want Clark in your house anymore, just say the word."

"He can stay. Look, until I can't go out there, let's just hold out hope, okay?"

"There you go," Clark said, leaning forward to give him a high five. "Just wait, man. We're gonna have sunburns all summer."

"Not me," Lisa said. "Melanoma is real and you're never too young to be vulnerable."

"She's chief of the sunscreen police, by the way."

"I didn't choose to be this person," Lisa defended. "It chose me."

"Good," Solomon added, standing up. "I knew the second I met you that you'd save my life someday."

PART TWO

SUMMER—ONE MONTH LATER

SEVENTEEN

SOLOMON REED

Summer didn't mean much to Solomon. He still did the same amount of schoolwork, a plan he'd discovered would save him an entire year of high school. If he worked all through each summer, he'd have the credits to get his diploma just after he turned seventeen. But, since meeting Clark and Lisa, he'd started slacking off a bit. It was an easy thing, being distracted by the two of them. And they made it easier by showing up nearly every day.

It wasn't always both of them, either. Lisa, being in Student Council *and* on the yearbook staff, was suddenly swamped at the end of the school year. So Clark started coming over without her. At first, Lisa made a big deal out of it—calling Solomon one afternoon, using that calm voice of hers, and explaining how busy she'd be over the following weeks. Eventually, Solomon just had to cut her off.

"Of course Clark can come over without you."

"I know, but I had to make sure. What if you secretly hate him and you've just been hanging out with him for me or something?"

"Is that the impression you get?"

"Yesterday, you guys spent two hours writing a theme song for a board game. I think you're probably the best friend he's ever had."

"It's a great song."

It seemed a little strange at first, but things weren't too different with Lisa gone. Solomon noticed, though, that every time she did have a chance to come over, she seemed distracted, always sitting quietly and watching as he and Clark talked about all the things she thought were stupid. Sometimes Solomon wondered if she was filming a Teenage Boys in their Natural Habitats documentary in her head.

It was good that they'd gotten used to her absence, because as soon as school was out for summer, Lisa had to go to Camp Elizabeth. It sounded like Solomon's own personal hell, complete with knot-tying classes and wilderness survival training. And the few times Lisa talked about it, she hadn't seemed all that thrilled either. Apparently she'd been guilted into it by her friend Janis, who Solomon was forbidden to meet.

"She'll try to pour holy water on you."

"Never mind."

Clark worked summers as a lifeguard at the Upland Community Center Pool. He hated it because his shift was from six a.m. to eleven a.m., five days a week. Sometimes, when he'd come over to Solomon's after work, he'd fall asleep on the couch. There were even a few afternoons when he'd be right in the middle of a sentence and doze off completely. So, Solomon would just read a book or watch TV until he woke up.

"I want to quit so bad," Clark said one day. "I feel like a zombie."

"So just hang out here. All the food and Netflix you can stand and a swimming pool on the way."

"Mom won't let me," he said.

"Well, if you don't spend money, you don't need it, right?"

"Yeah. It's not just that, though. She wants me to learn responsibility or something. And it's good for college applications."

"Lisa's worried you won't go."

"To college?" Clark asked. "I *may* not. I don't know yet."

"What else would you do?"

"That is also something I don't know yet."

"So, what's something you're good at? Aside from speaking made-up languages?"

"Swimming," he said. "But I'm not good enough to make a career out of it."

"That sucks. Are you sure?"

"It would be a very short career. And then what?"

"Maybe you can get paid to play video games or something. Don't they need people for that?"

"Oh no," he said. "I don't want my favorite thing to be my job. That would be a nightmare. No thank you."

"But you'd get paid to do what you love," Solomon argued.

"And what if that makes me stop loving it? I can't take the risk, man."

"My dad loves building things and he loves movies, so he builds movie sets. That's badass, right?"

"He *does* seem happy," Clark said. "But, like, what are the chances someone would just hire me to play games all day? I wish that were realistic but I'm sure it's a tough job to land."

"I wonder if I'll ever have a job," Solomon said.

"You could work online I guess."

"If I never get better, you mean?"

"Oh. No . . . I just . . ."

"Hey, I've accepted it. Maybe it sounds crazy to you, but that backyard may be the farthest I ever go."

"Do you ever think about being out there again? Like all the way out there?"

"I didn't use to," he said. "Not much anyway. Just the thought of it would give me a panic attack."

"And now?"

"It's still terrifying. But I can at least talk about it without crying, so that's a win."

"Well, maybe you could just picture being with us, huh? Like if we're out there with you, then it won't be so scary."

Solomon had good days and he had bad days, but the good had far outnumbered the bad since Lisa and Clark had started coming around. Sometimes, though, they'd show up and he'd look completely exhausted, drained of all his charm and moving in slow motion. They could do that to him—the attacks. Something about the physical response to panic can drain all the energy out of a person, and it doesn't matter what causes it or how long it lasts. What Solomon had was unforgiving and sneaky and as smart as any other illness. It was like a virus or cancer that would hide just long enough to fool him into thinking it was gone. And because it showed up when it damn well pleased, he'd learned to be honest about it, knowing that embarrassment only made it worse.

"Clark," he'd say. "Feeling loopy."

It was the best way to describe it. *Loopy.* Anxiety works a little differently for everyone, but it certainly always comes with cycling thoughts. Looping images that you can't control or stop, not easily anyway. Sometimes Solomon would start thinking about one of his parents dying. And then it would turn into both of them dying. And before he knew it, thoughts of something tragic happening to them—a car wreck, a random shooting, an earthquake—would swirl around in his mind so fast and so heavy that the only thing he could do was clench his fists and try to breathe as slowly as possible to not let it get to him, to not lose control the way he had so many times before.

Clark's way of dealing with it was to become a master at distraction therapy, which didn't work every time, but was always appreciated. When Solomon seemed particularly anxious, he'd try his best to keep his friend busy and over time, it seemed to be working.

"We need a project," Clark suggested the day Lisa left for camp.

"You're right. I can't play one more card game or I'll freak out."

"You know anything about cars?"

"What do you think?"

"I think that was a dumb question," he said. "Does your dad?"

"I don't know. Probably. Yours doesn't?"

"I've been asking him to help me fix up that van for six months and he still hasn't done it. So, I give up."

"What's wrong with it?"

"Well, it's a total piece of shit. I paid three hundred bucks for it last November and, honestly, I can't believe it hasn't blown up yet. I'm too scared to take it on the freeway because sometimes when I go over fifty, it starts smoking."

"That can't be good."

"I need to clean it out, too. It smells like wet socks and I think there's something dead in the back, but I'm too afraid to look. Lisa won't even ride in it anymore."

Solomon walked over to the kitchen window to look at Clark's van in the driveway. It was painted dark green, not professionally, and just on the side facing him, it had two hubcaps that didn't match and what looked like a mostly flat tire.

"Can you back it into the garage?"

"You mean the holodeck?" Clark asked, sounding offended.

"It won't hurt anything," Solomon said. "I can't help you fix it, but I can help you clean it out. And then maybe my dad can have a look at the engine when he gets home."

A few minutes later, with just the one single, dingy lightbulb casting its faint glow all over the garage, Clark climbed into the back of the van. It was disgusting, to say the least, so Solomon stood just outside of it, holding open a large black garbage bag with his face turned away.

"You okay?" Clark asked, amused.

"Just make it quick and don't throw any dead body parts at me."

"What about live body parts?"

Half an hour in, Solomon was tying up the first trash bag and walking into the house to get a second. He ran into his dad in the kitchen and nearly jumped out of his skin.

"Holy shit!" he yelled.

"Watch your mouth," his dad said. "Who are you, your mother? What're you up to anyway?"

"We're cleaning out Clark's van."

"Clark's here?"

"He's in the garage."

His dad followed him back and helped hold the trash bag while Clark tossed in soda cans, crumpled fast-food bags, and weird random things like a ripped pair of blue jean shorts and a deflated basketball.

"Are you teen wolf, Clark?" Solomon's dad asked.

"Only on the weekends."

They eventually took a break to have dinner, something Clark stayed for most nights of the week now. Valerie loved it, feeling like she had two fully functioning sons instead of one that just got by. Of course she didn't say it aloud like that, but Solomon was smart enough to see it on her face. And he saw it on his dad's, too. They hadn't made it to dessert before Clark had convinced him to take a look at the van. By midnight, Jason was covered in oil and grease from his elbows to his fingertips. He'd been picking around the motor and listing things they needed to get it running right. Solomon jotted down everything his dad said, contributing the only way he knew how. But, mostly, he watched Clark as he nodded his head to these very technical things Jason was describing and pretended not to be clueless.

"You may need a new carburetor," his dad said.

"Right, right," Clark agreed. "Totally."

And maybe it was because Lisa had been gone for so long or because fumes were leaking from the van's potentially toxic motor, but that was the night Solomon realized how he really felt about Clark Robbins. He'd ignored it for weeks—that feeling he got in his stomach when Clark was around, that rushing in his chest that he'd mistaken for panic so many times, but had actually been something else, something he hadn't felt before. Clark didn't care where he was or where he was going. And even though Solomon was afraid to call it love, what else could it be? It was there. It was real. And if he didn't watch out, it would eventually find a way to ruin everything.

EIGHTEEN
LISA PRAYTOR

Summer camp had been so much fun when Lisa was younger. She'd get to meet interesting girls from faraway places like Phoenix or Salt Lake City and their cabins would come up with secret little languages and songs about the wilderness. But as she grew older, and reached that pivotal age where being a counselor was her only choice, Lisa found herself constantly nostalgic for the way it once was.

Now, as a junior counselor, she was in charge of her own cabin, complete with ten girls and one senior counselor. That senior counselor was Janis. And she had a hard time forgetting that *this* camp, one of the three she counseled at every summer, wasn't a Christian one like the other two.

"Let us pray," she said on the third night just before lights-out.

"Keep it secular," Lisa whispered from the bunk beneath her.

"I mean . . . sweet dreams, campers."

The first week of camp went by pretty quietly, with only

one canoe mishap and no reports of stomach bugs from the other bunks. And even though she wondered how Clark and Solomon were doing without her, Lisa was having fun being around some other girls for a change. She hadn't heard the words *Star Trek* in seven days and it felt amazing.

The only thing that was a little off was Janis. Lisa knew it wouldn't be easy, but she'd thought setting aside her very important time with Solomon to come to camp last minute would put the things back to normal between them. She was wrong. Janis was still pouting about it, constantly making little jokes about Lisa disappearing or being flaky. She kept her mouth shut, not wanting to argue in front of the young campers, but now Lisa was starting to get pissed. Still, though, she knew the last week of camp would be much easier if she tried to keep the peace—at least for as long as Janis would let her.

"Listen," Lisa said, sitting down across from Janis in the mess hall, "we've got to talk to Chloe. If she doesn't learn to steer a canoe, she'll have to take the class all over again next summer."

"Lisa, just do it for her. We're not training her for the Olympics."

"I can't do that and you know it. Where's your Camp Elizabeth pride?"

"Sorry. But, the girl's hopeless. She sunk three canoes and a kayak last summer."

"Oh, I remember that."

"So, are you having a good time? Glad you came?" Janis asked blandly.

"Maybe," Lisa said.

"It was the least you could do, really."

"What's that supposed to mean?"

"You know exactly what it means," Janis said. "Plus, I'm trying to save you from that crazy kid. I'm sure you needed a break."

"He's not crazy," she said. "And I do *not* need you to save me from anything."

"You know, maybe I'm too normal to be your friend. Not enough problems for you to fix, Lisa?"

"You've got plenty of problems, believe me."

Janis was completely caught off guard that Lisa had finally stood up for herself. She leaned closer, putting her palms on the table, and with that mean look in her eyes, the one she used to get before she found Jesus, Janis smiled a little before she began to speak.

"Don't take out all your anger on me. I can't help it if your boyfriend's in love with that crazy kid. I tried to warn you."

"You're ridiculous."

"You act so smart, Lisa. You're always talking about how you want to help people and become this amazing psychiatrist someday, but you can't even see what's going on right in front of you. Where do you think Clark is right now?"

"He's with his friend. *Our* friend. Don't make stuff up just because you're jealous."

"All right. I'm out," Janis said loudly, throwing her hands up.

"You're *out*?"

"That's right. Have fun wrangling Cabin Twelve all by yourself."

Janis stormed off and Lisa was left standing outside the mess hall with a group of young campers staring right at her. She flashed them a forced smile and walked back inside to get some lunch. She kept that same smile on her face all day, taking on the role of two counselors until the camp leaders could shuffle someone around to help her. Janis had stormed right to the head counselor's office and demanded she be moved to another cabin. Lisa was sure Janis had told some lie about her to make it easier. But, what good would it do to go tell them the truth? At least now she wouldn't have to be reminded of how bad a friend she was every fifteen minutes for the rest of camp.

Later that evening, as the campers were eating dinner and watching the camp improv group, two other counselors, Tara and Lydia, sat down beside Lisa with a hungry look in their eyes like they always got when gossip was floating around camp.

"I heard she called you a bitch. Is that what happened?" Tara whispered.

"No, I told you. She called her boyfriend gay," Lydia added.

"She did? Why would she do that?" Tara asked.

"Will you two shut up?" Lisa said, her whisper a little louder than theirs. "It's not a big deal. She's just jealous."

"I heard your boyfriend's been spending all his time with a gay guy," Lydia said. "Is that true?"

"They're like best friends," Lisa defended. "He's my friend, too. There's nothing wrong with it."

"Do they hang out without you?" Tara asked.

"Of course."

Then Tara and Lydia quickly shot each other a look and turned back to her with sad eyes.

"Are you okay?" Lydia asked.

"Damn it. Will you two listen to me? My friend Sol is gay. My boyfriend Clark isn't. I know, because he's my boyfriend. So drop it and please *stop* listening to Janis."

"Just let me ask you this," Tara said. "Do you have sex?"

"*That* would be none of your business."

"Just answer the question," Lydia ordered.

"We've come close a few times."

"Oh, no," Tara gasped, shaking her head.

"You poor thing," Lydia added.

Lisa gave them a blank stare and then fixed her eyes on the performance stage, pretending they weren't beside her. Janis had gotten to them first—probably to everyone first—so now Lisa was the girl at Camp Elizabeth with the gay boyfriend, no matter how much she denied it. Gossip works that way. It makes fools out of everyone but the source. Lisa was relieved, though, that Janis hadn't told them about the essay. Maybe that meant she hadn't completely lost her oldest friend for good.

That night, she lay awake for a while after lights-out, following a firefly that had found its way into the cabin as it floated and hovered above her. She wondered if Clark was at Solomon's. She couldn't help picturing them together.

Janis and the other counselors had somehow etched it into her brain like a drunken tattoo—something that should've never been there, but was impossible to erase. And no matter how many times she convinced herself that it couldn't be true, she still kept coming back around to the possibility that it could.

NINETEEN
SOLOMON REED

The day before they finally put water in the pool, Solomon called Lisa hyperventilating. Since she'd gotten home from camp the night before, he was hoping she'd come over and convince him that going into the backyard wouldn't make the world end. And as he listened to her calm voice reassuring him, he felt a pang of guilt for kind of liking it. Maybe this was just his version of getting better, of accepting that sometimes he needed help. He'd missed her, especially the way she took charge of things. If he couldn't be in control, he knew she could, and without her, things were starting to get weird.

"You hear about the van?" Solomon asked a while after he'd calmed down. "That thing is part of my home now."

"Your dad can't fix it?"

"I know my dad," he said. "And the look on his face when he's out there taking that motor apart tells me he doesn't have a clue what he's doing."

"That's hilarious," Lisa said.

"It is, isn't it?"

"It doesn't matter that much to Clark," she said. "I think he just wanted another reason to hang out with you."

"You think so? Because I'm in such high demand socially, right?"

"What did you do while I was gone? Besides taking a van apart."

"Same ole same ole," he said. "TV, games, watched a movie or two."

"Clark said you started *Lost* again."

"Yeah. We're on Season Two. I think it's better the second time."

"I wish you guys had waited for me."

"Oh. I'm sorry."

"It's okay. I can jump in, I've got a good memory anyway."

"Sweet. So, tell me I can do this again."

"You *can* do it, Sol. You've been waiting months for this pool and all you have to do now is remember how that water will feel as you're gliding through it."

"Gliding?"

"I'm trying to be inspirational," she said.

"Sorry."

"Remember that it's no different from being inside. Nothing can happen out there that can't happen in your house."

"I could drown."

"It *has* been a while since you've gone swimming, I guess."

"A *long* while."

"Do you want us there? We should be there, right?"

"I don't know," he said. "Part of me thinks it would help, but another part of me doesn't want a bigger audience to disappoint."

"It's not like that," she said.

"It is, though. It is. And you guys would have the right to be disappointed. I want to just say *yes, I can go outside and get in that pool*, but I can't yet. I won't know until tomorrow."

"I think you'll be fine," she said. "I really do."

"Okay. Here's an idea. I want you guys there, but you have to promise to swim. Even if I can't. Maybe that'll distract my parents from the heartache."

"Promise," she said. "I'll talk to Clark."

"Awesome."

"No matter what, you'll finally get to see those abs in person. They're majestic."

"Can I tell you a secret? I've been doing crunches for weeks so I won't be too embarrassed."

"That's hilarious. How's that working for you?"

"I don't have the muscle," he said. "He really is from Krypton, isn't he?"

"Superman would never drive that van," she said. "Hey, does he ever talk about me?"

"Are you kidding? When is he *not* talking about you?"

"Be serious," she said. "I want to know if he talks about me. Good or bad. Just tell me."

"Lisa, he talks about you all the time. Always good. What's wrong?"

"Nothing. Just missing the gang, I guess. You down for some company?"

"You know the answer to that," he said. "We also have a Munchkin tournament to finish."

"Yes, we do. Clark's at work, so we'll be over around five, okay?"

That afternoon, as soon as they pulled into the driveway and got out of Lisa's car, Solomon swung open the front door wearing a plastic Viking helmet and holding up a toy sword.

"Tonight, we dine in hell!" he yelled as they walked up.

"We must have the wrong house," Lisa said.

"Prepare to be slaughtered!" Clark yelled, running past her and into the doorway, where he grabbed the sword and pointed it toward her.

"Good luck," she said. "I brought my A game today, boys. It's going to be rough."

"She's got to go down," Clark said as she strutted by him.

Halfway into the first game, neither of them had a snowball's chance in hell of beating her. Three games later, she was still undefeated. When the tournament was finally over, Solomon threw his cards down in fake anger and Clark fell to the floor like she'd stabbed him in the heart.

"Who wants a rematch?" Lisa said maniacally.

"I need a break," Solomon said. "I thought I really missed you until this bloodbath."

"What are they teaching you at summer camp?" Clark asked.

"The only thing I learned is that Janis is sort of a bitch and Sloppy Joes are still disgusting."

"I can't believe you won't let me meet her," Solomon said. "She sounds so . . . fun."

"I think she hates me," Clark added.

"Who could hate you?" Solomon asked.

"I know, right?" Clark stood up and walked over to the sliding glass door. He looked out at the backyard and then turned toward Solomon.

"You ready for tomorrow?" he asked.

"Don't know."

Solomon got up and walked over to stand beside him. He gazed out at the empty pool, half filled with moonlight and half with darkness. And the only thing he could think about was how useless it was without water—just a weird-shaped concrete hole in the backyard.

"Maybe you should go out there tonight," Lisa said.

"What? Why?"

"Your parents aren't home. So *that* pressure's off. Maybe we all just walk right outside like it's nothing."

"Like it's nothing?" Solomon asked. "It's not nothing."

"I know," she said. "But we can make it nothing, Sol. Let's make it nothing."

She walked over and reached for his hand. For a second, he thought about giving it to her, about letting her drag him out there and getting it over with. *Pull it like a Band-Aid*, his grandma would say. But he couldn't.

"Not tonight, Lisa."

"Tomorrow then," Clark said, quickly patting Solomon's right shoulder with one hand. "It's going to be great, buddy."

Solomon couldn't sleep that night. He wished it were like Christmas when he was a kid—that nervous excitement keeping him up in anticipation of a living room full of new toys and gadgets. But it was more like an aching pit in his stomach, a deep, low pain that pulsated all night and constantly reminded him of what the next day would bring.

At three in the morning, he tiptoed down the hallway in just a pair of pajama pants. He stepped into the living room, staring at the sliding glass door like he was staring deep into the void of space, a black hole leading into a world that had been so far out of his reach for so long. He moved closer, close enough to grip the door handle. Close enough to see his breath on the glass. And then he slid it open.

He didn't move. But the cool early morning breeze swirled around in his face, lifting patches of his shaggy hair, and making him shiver. He wasn't going to cry or anything. And he didn't feel anxious or especially loopy, either. He was so close to the outside, but he was still standing, and that helped his breathing even out a bit. His heartbeat was strong, but not frantic like all the other times he'd secretly tried to go out there. All those times he'd never told anyone about. Now it was different, though. He was ready. And the pain in his stomach was starting to go away. So he just went for it.

He stepped outside. And then he kept going, until he was walking down the pool steps and into the deep end. When he got there, where the drain sat brand-new and ready, he lay down on the faux-pebble surface and looked up at the stars.

And that's where they found him sleeping the next morning.

TWENTY
LISA PRAYTOR

Most people her age wouldn't have been awake at eight thirty a.m. when Solomon called the next day, but Lisa wasn't like most people. She'd already showered, gotten dressed, straightened her hair, *and* had a bagel with cream cheese. Sleeping in was for the unmotivated.

"You're up early," she answered.

"Guess where I am."

"Very funny."

"No, really. Guess."

"Your bedroom?"

"I'm in the backyard, Lisa."

"Shut your mouth."

"I won't. I can't. I'm outside. It's nice out here, right?"

"Oh my God, Sol."

"Listen to me. I'm okay. Why aren't you over here yet? Where's Clark?"

"Is there even any water in the pool?"

"They just started filling it up. Said we could swim at five or six. I'm not sure I can make it that long."

"Wait, you're outside right now?"

"Yeah, sitting in the grass. I didn't realize I missed doing this."

"Wow . . . this is . . ."

"It was weird. I couldn't sleep. At all. So in the middle of the night, I just opened the door and walked out here."

"Amazing."

"I fell asleep in the pool."

"You what?"

"Dad found me before he left for work. I've never seen him so happy."

"I can imagine," she said. "I bet your mom cried."

"She was already at work. But I'm sure she'll attack me when she gets home."

"This is so great, Sol. How do you feel right now?"

"Like I passed the entrance exam for Starfleet Academy."

"I'm going to guess that means good."

"I feel awesome. Did you know you can hear the free-way from my backyard?"

"Mine too," she said. "I'm going to call and wake Clark up and then head over. Don't get tired of being outside before we get there."

"Yeah, right."

Lisa couldn't get Clark on the phone, so she drove over to his mom's and banged on the door until someone answered. It was Drew and she was not happy to be awake.

"Lisa?" she said, sleepy-eyed.

"Hey, sorry. Is he here?" She stepped around her and walked down the hallway toward his room. She thought about knocking, but she didn't. She walked right in and found him asleep with one leg hanging over the side of the bed and his face completely covered by a blanket.

"Clark?" she whispered loudly. He didn't move. "Clark!"

He shot up and out of the bed so fast that Lisa jumped back, afraid he'd start swinging his fists or something. Then she laughed and looked him up and down.

"Clark, you're naked."

"Shit. Sorry." He grabbed the blanket and wrapped it around himself. Then he sat down on the bed.

"*This* I did not know about you," she said. "Must get cold."

"What time is it?"

"Eight forty-five. I know it's early, but Sol went outside."

"What?"

"Yeah. He just called me. We have to go see this."

"Okay. Right. Umm . . . don't look."

He quickly stood up and slid on a pair of boxers that was lying on the floor. Lisa pretended not to look, but it had been a while since she'd been alone with him and even longer since she'd seen this much of his body.

"I mean, we could wait fifteen minutes or so," she said suggestively, reaching over to grab his wrist.

"Are you kidding me?" He pulled his arm away. "He's *outside*. We've gotta get over there."

With a defeated look on her face, Lisa watched as he threw on a pair of shorts and a T-shirt. Then, just as she stood up to follow him out, he turned back and gave her a huge smile.

"I need swim trunks, don't I?"

"Yeah," she said. "And sunscreen."

On the drive over, Clark couldn't stop talking about how proud he was of their friend. He used words like *pumped*

and *psyched* and every time he said Solomon's name, Lisa
felt a little pang of jealousy. He'd just had the chance to
sleep with his girlfriend and instead he was going on and
on about someone else. Lisa had created this monster, but
she no longer had any control over it.

"I told you it would work," she said.

"You're joking, right?" Clark asked, rolling his eyes.

"But, look what it's done," she defended. "He's outside.
It's only a matter of time before he goes even farther."

"Okay, Dr. Praytor," he said with sarcasm.

Lisa thought he was joking, but the second she went to
speak again, she noticed the serious look on his face and
stopped herself. The rest of the ride was silent, with Lisa
staring straight ahead at the road and Clark looking down
at his phone. When they pulled up in the driveway, she
turned to him and didn't have to say anything for him to
respond.

"Lisa, hear me out. If you write that essay, I'm telling
him," he said, never looking her way as he got out of the car.

When they stepped into the backyard, there he was,
wearing a pair of sunglasses and lying back on a lounge
chair, his arms up over his head. Lisa hadn't seen Solomon
without a shirt on before and she could definitely tell he
hadn't lied about all those crunches. Clark ran across the
yard and started lifting Solomon up off the chair to give
him a hug.

"Look what this guy's been hiding!" he yelled to Lisa,
pointing at Solomon's pale, bare torso.

"You're going to be a lobster," she said. "Do you have
sunscreen on?"

"I do. I swear," Solomon answered.

Clark lifted up one of Solomon's arms and smelled it.

"He's lying," he said. "Here, we brought some."

"Thanks." Solomon rubbed the sunscreen on his arms and then Lisa walked over to help him get his back.

"If you die of skin cancer, we won't have anywhere to swim," she said.

They sat outside watching the pool slowly fill with water. Solomon didn't seem to be tired of the sun yet, so they figured they'd stay out there for as long as he wanted. And every time he got up and walked to a new part of the yard, Lisa watched him like he was an astronaut walking around on some distant planet, his every step further proof that anything is possible.

"How much longer?" Solomon asked them, nearly shouting from the other side of the yard. It looked like he'd been inspecting the flowers under his parents' window, but Lisa wasn't sure.

"Well," Clark said loudly, "with a hose that size, about five-eighths of an inch in diameter, you're delivering seventeen gallons of water per minute, which is one thousand twenty gallons an hour, so . . . with a five-thousand-gallon pool, it should take about five more hours."

"What the hell?" Solomon asked, walking up to them.

"He read it off his phone," Lisa said.

Clark held up his phone and gave Solomon a big smile. Then he hopped up onto his feet and told them to pose for a picture.

"We have to document this important day in history," he said.

Solomon bent down and put one arm around Lisa's shoulders. This was the most he'd ever touched her and she couldn't help but flinch a little out of shock.

"Sorry," he said, pulling away.

"No." She grabbed his arm to keep it in place.

Clark had been taking pictures of the three of them for weeks, but he usually tried to keep it as subtle as possible, quickly snapping a shot of Lisa and Solomon as they looked down at their cards or watched TV. Lisa noticed every time, though, and now she wondered what she'd find on his phone from all the days she'd spent away. Surely he wouldn't have taken photos of Solomon all by himself. That would be strange, wouldn't it? But, even if he did, then so what? Friends take pictures of their friends all the time. It was perfectly normal. She didn't need to check his phone. That wouldn't help anything. It was all so stupid. Janis had really gotten to her, and she was starting to find it a bit more aggravating than it was amusing.

"Hey," she said. "Let's go in and eat something, huh? Sol, can you sacrifice a few minutes of daylight. Don't want to get too tired of it on day one."

"I guess," he said, faking disappointment. "I'm starving anyway."

"I want peanut butter and jelly," Clark said. "All of it. All of it that's in the world."

"My mom buys extra for him," Solomon told Lisa.

Then Clark froze just outside of the door and turned to face them.

"You're not going to be stuck again if we go inside are you?"

"Dude," Solomon said, stepping past him and through the doorway. "I've been doing this all day. Relax."

Once inside, they made their way to the kitchen, where she listened to the two of them banter back and forth about how to make the perfect pb&j. They both had it all wrong. You've got to stir the peanut butter and jelly together before applying it to the bread. Then they sort of ventured off into their own little world and left Lisa sitting there to watch, unable to get a word in edgewise.

Maybe that was her fault, for all the time she'd spent quietly observing them and studying Solomon's tics and triggers. It was like they spoke a language she'd only just forgotten. She could pick up on some of their references, but mostly found herself completely lost in their jargon.

So, Lisa eventually stopped trying to understand them and let her mind drift back to her conversation with Clark. She knew he'd probably never forgive her if she wrote that essay. But, she also knew she had to. It was a surefire way to save herself and she was too close to give up now. Just as Solomon needed to leave the house, Lisa needed to leave Upland. He was better. She did that. She deserved to get out, too.

TWENTY-ONE
SOLOMON REED

For Solomon, swimming was the opposite of a panic attack. Fluid and calm and quiet. The world was muffled just enough when he went under, and the way the wind felt on his wet skin when he came up for air made him forget he was closer to all the things that scared him so much and had for so long.

As he got into the pool for the first time, his family and friends looking on in silence, he felt like he could cry. And he did, but just a little, and to avoid it being a big deal, he fell face-first into the water and then came up smiling. After that, he wouldn't stop swimming long enough for anyone to ask if he was okay. But, of course he was. Nothing worked like the water.

When Solomon's dad cannonballed into the pool, he waded over to his son and made a big show out of trying to kiss him on the forehead. And all his mom could do was take pictures, this look in her eyes like she was documenting a miracle. Finally, after they'd been begging her for an hour, she got in the pool and joined them for Marco Polo.

"He'll never get him," Solomon said to his mom and

Lisa. They were all sitting on the edge of the pool in the shallow end by the stairs, an area Solomon's dad had designated as the Loser Zone. He'd caught all three of them but hadn't even gotten close to Clark once.

He drifted slowly through the water like an alligator watching its prey, his nose above the surface just enough to breathe and the rest of him hidden underneath. He'd let Solomon's dad get close enough to touch him and he'd answer *Polo* in a whisper then sort of magically float right by him to one side. He was taunting him and every time he *did* hold his face out of the water, he'd shoot a huge grin over toward his audience.

Solomon, Clark, and Lisa stayed in the pool long enough to see the sun set and slowly watch the moon creep up to the center of the sky. They only got out to eat, pee, or when their fingers turned so pruney they started aching. Around ten, after Solomon's parents had gone to bed, the three of them lay side by side, Solomon in the middle, with their feet in the water and their backs resting on the cold, pebbly ground that surrounded the pool.

"If this were an indie movie, we'd start talking about the constellations," Solomon said, looking up at the stars.

"I always thought *Ursa Major* would be a cool name," Clark said. "Hi, I'm Ursa Major Robbins. Nice to meet you."

"Ursa Major Reed, Attorney at Law," Solomon added. "God, I missed this view."

"It is pretty damn good, isn't it?" Lisa said.

At midnight, they finally said good-bye. He walked them to the front door, a towel around his waist and his half-wet hair sticking up and out in all directions. Lisa kissed him on the cheek and whispered into his ear. *I'm so proud of you*, she said. Then Clark attacked him with a bear hug that raised him off his feet. And, despite it hurting his mildly sunburned arms, that was the best hug of his life.

Once they were gone, he walked back outside and sat by the pool. There were no lights on in the backyard except for the one that shone from the deep end and cast a whitish-blue glow all over Solomon's skin. He dipped his feet in the water, watching ripples as they moved out in tiny little glowing waves and he closed his eyes to listen to the only sound he could hear, water lapping against the side of the pool.

He thought about sleeping out there again, curling up on a lounge chair and letting the daylight wake him. He'd missed the sun, realizing now how stupid it had been to think he could live without it. He felt a pang of guilt as he looked around the backyard, tracing the top of the wooden fence with his eyes. Maybe he could've been coming out here this whole time. It felt so easy now. All it took was one step and it was like it had never been off limits, like he hadn't gone three years without touching the grass or feeling the sun on his skin or shivering in the night breeze. Is this what getting better felt like? And if all he had to do was close his eyes and take a step to make everything better, then why couldn't he just do it? Just rip it like a Band-Aid. Why did the thought of walking out that front door still make him feel like his heart was imploding?

"This is all I need," he said aloud into the darkness of the yard. But even he wasn't sure he believed it anymore.

. . .

The next day, Solomon woke up to the sound of his grandma's voice echoing down the hall and into his bedroom. His parents were at work, so he knew she was on the phone with a client or something, probably being intentionally loud to wake him up.

When he walked into the kitchen a few minutes later, she was sitting at the counter with her reading glasses barely on the tip of her nose and a newspaper in her hands. For a minute she didn't see him, so she kept reading and humming to herself.

"Grandma?"

She threw the paper down, jumped up, and ran across the kitchen to hug him. She planted a big, loud kiss on the side of his face and then squeezed him again, so tight she took the wind out of his lungs.

"Okay, okay," he said, backing up. "You're freaking me out."

"Look at you! You've already got a tan!"

"It's a sunburn."

"Sunburn schmunburn. You look alive, kid. Like somebody brought you back from the dead."

"Thanks," he said. "You bring your swimsuit? The pool's awesome."

"No, no. I've got three houses to show by five. I just came to see it for myself."

"The pool?"

"Are you kidding? I've seen thousands of pools, Solomon. I want to see you out there. Go on. Start walking. I'm very busy."

When he stepped out into the backyard, she did the hug and loud kiss thing all over again. He thanked her for the pool, but she wouldn't hear it, choosing instead to take pictures of him standing in the grass and by the fence and sitting on the diving board. By the time she was done, his face was sore from all the smiling.

"I missed the mountains," he said, pointing over into the distance.

"I never liked 'em," she said. "Don't get it."

"Really? I love them."

"Yeah, well, I always wanted to live by the beach when I moved out here. I did, for a while, you know? Back when I was trying to be an actress some girlfriends and I got a place in Long Beach. It wasn't as nice back then, but we could afford it and it was close enough to the city to carpool to casting calls and our real jobs—waitressing."

"So why'd you move out here then?"

"Your grandpa. This was his hometown and he wasn't going to live anywhere else. He made that very clear when we met, and despite my better judgment, I married him anyway."

"You know you loved him," he said. "Why're you always talking trash about Grandpa?"

"Tell you a secret?"

"Yeah."

"Makes it easier. If I pretend all he did was drive me crazy, I don't miss him so much. It works. Maybe it's bad, but it works."

"I wish I'd met him."

"He would've loved you. You're . . . like he was. He kept

to himself, mostly, but when you caught him in the right mood, he'd talk for hours. He'd tell stories till he was blue in the face—*did you hear the one about* whatever. I see that in your dad sometimes, too."

"Three generations of crazy."

"A loony legacy" she said.

"A straight coat of arms."

"You win."

"Are you going to make me swim, too?" he asked. "I think my trunks are in the washer."

"No," she said. "Just promise me you won't drown in this nice expensive pool while no one's here all day, okay? Don't give me *that* to live with for the next twenty years."

"I bet you've got more than twenty."

"Shhh," she snapped. "I'm a dinosaur. Give me a hug so I can go earn your inheritance back."

Once he was alone, he didn't bother going to get his trunks. Instead he walked back to the pool, threw his pjs and T-shirt onto the ground, and jumped right in. He swam around for a while, sometimes breaking to float on his back and get warm from the sun before diving back down to the bottom and turning flips all the way back up. He hadn't heard the doorbell inside, so he had the absolute shit scared out of him when he popped up from the water to take a big breath and Clark Robbins was standing at the edge of the pool with a huge smile on his face.

"Holy shit!" Solomon yelled, quickly covering his privates with both hands and going back underwater.

He thought maybe it was all a hallucination, some weird effect of all this swimming after so many years without it. But he opened his eyes and looked up to see the cloudy image of his friend looking down at him. Then, just as he was about to come up for air, Clark jumped in.

When his head was above water, he saw Clark's clothes, *all* of his clothes, lying on the ground. He looked over where he'd jumped in and watched the shiny figure swim down toward the bottom. He was too embarrassed and paranoid to stick his head underwater and try for a better view, but he did consider it.

When Clark's head popped up by the diving board, he looked right at Solomon and smiled.

"Don't judge. It's effing cold in here."

"I'm not *looking*," Solomon said quickly. "How'd you get in?"

"Door was unlocked," he said, starting to swim closer.

"Weird."

It was the first time Solomon had ever forgotten to lock the front door. Ever. And if very naked Clark hadn't been swimming toward him, he would've had time to freak out about *that*, too.

"So this whole ploy . . . this swimming pool thing was just so you could skinny-dip, huh?"

"For sure," Solomon said. "Caught me. I'll go get my trunks in a second."

"Nobody here but us."

"Lisa?"

"Said she wasn't feeling well. Told me to keep you company."

Solomon, still naked, still covering his business with both hands, eyed his towel where it sat impossibly far away on a chair. Clark was just swimming around the pool behind him like everything was normal.

Solomon stayed in one spot for a while, unable to move, too embarrassed and confused and overwhelmed to do anything but try to seem like he wasn't watching Clark. But how could he not be watching him? He was naked and swimming all around him. It was like every gay dude's dream come true—a naked athlete floating around in the backyard. Or maybe it was just Solomon's dream with this particular athlete. Either way, it was happening and his eyes didn't know where to go.

"Hey," Clark said, swimming up way too close to him. "You're blushing."

"Sunburn," he said, trying his best not to look down.

"I'll go get my shorts."

Clark used both hands to pull himself out of the water and Solomon watched as he walked across the yard, his bare white butt right there for all the neighborhood to see. He took his swim trunks off the fence where he'd left them drying the night before.

And since Clark was looking the other way, Solomon quickly climbed out of the pool and wrapped a nearby towel around his waist.

"I'm going to go grab mine," he said, walking across yard and into the house.

When he returned, Clark was in the water doing a handstand. He waited for him to come up for air before jumping

back in and then he swam to the shallow end and took a
seat on one of the steps.

"You okay, man?" Clark asked, wading toward him.

"Yeah," he said unconvincingly. "Totally."

"Hey, look, I'm used to the locker room and a house
with three brothers. I shouldn't have done that."

"It's not a big deal," he said. "I just . . . I don't know.
Sorry I'm being weird."

"Sol," Clark said, moving closer. "It's okay. You can
look, just don't touch."

"Jerk," he said, a smile forcing its way onto his face.

"Really, though. I'm sorry if I made you uncomfortable.
You're like my brother or something, I just didn't even
think twice about it."

Solomon went underwater, opened his eyes, and let the
words echo and sink in and swim all around in his head.
Like my brother.

He shook it off and challenged Clark to a race. Clark
won, of course, but Solomon came surprisingly close, especially for someone so out of practice. He also couldn't
help being distracted by Clark, watching him as he moved
through the water. He liked the way his hair looked when
it was wet, slicked back like an old movie star. And he
was fascinated by the little patch of dark hair Clark had
growing in the center of his chest.

"I didn't see that in your water polo pictures. The ones
Lisa showed me," Solomon said.

"I shave it during the season. Don't make fun."

"Hey, I can't even grow one hair on my chest. Respect."

"My dad looks like a grizzly bear with his shirt off. I'm so jealous," Clark said. "I want, like, caveman body hair, the kind that hovers all around you, you know? That's the manliest you can get."

"And *why* do you need to be so manly?"

"Well, she won't tell you, but it's Lisa's thing. She likes a real scruffy sort of guy. Maybe I should grow a beard."

"Lumbersexual," Solomon said. "I think that's what they call it."

"Nice," Clark said. "I want a beard and to be covered in body hair and then I'll marry Lisa and we'll move to Portland or something and build a tiny house."

"*That's* your dream?"

"I think so," Clark said, immediately following it with a backflip in the water.

Solomon got quiet after that, but he tried to talk just enough for Clark not to sense anything. He was so angry at himself for letting this happen, for feeling the way he felt about Clark. No matter how hard he tried, he couldn't shake it, either. And, long after Clark had gone home, Solomon stayed up wondering if everyone falls in love with someone who can't love them back.

TWENTY-TWO
LISA PRAYTOR

Lisa was pretending to be sick so she wouldn't have to spend another whole day watching Solomon Reed steal her boyfriend. And it was *that* kind of thinking that told her she needed to talk to someone. That someone had to be Janis. Not the Janis from camp—fueled by anger and jealousy—but the one she'd known her whole life who could sometimes suspend her self-righteousness just long enough to say all the right things.

As Lisa knocked on the door, she closed her eyes and turned her head to one side, almost hoping no one would answer.

"What?" Janis barked, swinging the door open.

"Hi."

"What do you want, Lisa?"

"We have to talk."

"No we don't."

Lisa knew what she had to do. The only way to reconcile with someone like Janis, who lived for drama, was to give her a good old-fashioned emotional breakdown. It was through tears that she got her real strength. And Lisa was ready to pay up.

So, she silently stepped forward and hugged Janis around the neck, putting as much of her weight on her shoulders as possible. Lisa was prepared to put on a performance, but she hadn't expected the floodgates to open like they did and before she knew it, she and Janis were both sobbing in each other's arms.

It didn't take long before they'd made up. They were more like sisters than either of them would ever admit, so they'd had their fair share of big blowups in the past. Lisa wanted to take Janis to lunch, so she waited while her friend got ready and then drove her to a sandwich place downtown. They sat outside and Lisa looked over the menu while Janis texted someone, her fingers furiously tapping her phone screen. Then she let out a big laugh and kept texting, completely ignoring Lisa and everything else around her.

"Who's that?" Lisa asked.

She set the phone facedown and gave her friend a big, sneaky smile.

"I thought you'd never ask. I have a boyfriend."

"A *what*? That's awesome!"

"His name's Trevor Blackwell. We met at Camp Christ Is Risen."

"Last year?"

"Yeah. But, he had a girlfriend, so I waited and prayed and then, a couple weeks ago, he messaged me and said they broke up. You've got to see him. He's like a model or something."

Janis picked her phone back up, clicked a few times, and handed it to Lisa. He was attractive enough, in that unassuming sort of way like the best friend in every movie you've ever seen. Lisa hammed it up, though.

"He's *so* cute, Janis. That smile. Maybe *I* should go to this camp."

"We met during a reenactment of the crucifixion."

"Your first date was a crucifixion?"

"Reenactment," Janis corrected. "It wasn't a date. It was love at first sight."

Lisa couldn't help imagining these lovebirds standing in the woods while two high schoolers pretended to whip a dude dressed like Jesus in the background.

"I'm glad, Janis. You seem really happy."

"I am," she said, grabbing her phone. "I just wish he lived closer."

"Where's he live?"

"Tustin. But it may as well be Jupiter."

"That's not *that* far," Lisa said. "Like an hour."

"An hour is an eternity when you're this in love. But, I'll see him at camp next week."

"Janis, please don't get knocked up at Christian camp."

"Can you imagine? My mom would kill me."

"You could always call it a miracle Virgin birth maybe?"

"Well, gosh, I hadn't thought of that."

After lunch, they went to a serve-yourself yogurt shop around the corner. It had been their spot once, after school and sometimes on Sundays. It was weird being there, after so long, and Lisa was feeling a little overwhelmed by Janis's nonstop talking.

"So, how are your boyfriends?" Janis asked.

"Good," she said. "Just . . . yeah . . . good."

"Look, I'm sorry for what I said, okay? It wasn't fair. And what do I know anyway?"

"Maybe you were right," Lisa said, louder than she intended, and then threw her head down to hide her face in her arms.

"What?"

"I think maybe I was wrong," she said, her face still covered.

"He's gay?" Janis asked, in a whisper, leaning down.

Lisa shot her head up and let herself slide down in the plastic chair.

"I don't know. He spends all his time with Sol. *All* his time. And when he's not doing that, he's talking about him or making plans with him. I didn't even realize it was happening and now I think it's too late."

"Well, you're born gay, so if it's true, it was too late a long time ago, Lisa."

"I guess so."

"Spending all their time together doesn't make them gay, either. It makes them . . . I don't know . . . two loners who found each other, maybe."

"True."

"So, you could be reading too much into it. You need to be sure before you do anything."

"What's there to do? I love him. He knows that. But it just feels weird between us now."

"Even if he was gay, would Clark lie to you?"

"Yeah. That's the part I can't figure out. Plus, even if he is lying, shouldn't I be supportive? I can't make him feel guilty about being who he really is."

"There's a difference in being yourself and cheating on someone. You think Clark would do that to you? And aren't you and Solomon close? Would *he* do that?"

"I don't think so," she said. "But what if they can't help it?"

"Then at least maybe you'll get your scholarship."

"I thought you *disapproved*?"

"I do. But, I mean . . . it's a unique perspective. Plus, you could get a lot of sympathy if you go for the whole *crazy kid stole my boyfriend* angle."

"Clark doesn't want me to do it. He said he'd tell Sol about the essay if I write it. Just another reason I think he cares more about him than he does me."

"No way," she said. "He's just doing the right thing."

"I know. So, maybe I just need to tell him, huh? Tell Solomon the truth and hope it doesn't reverse all the progress he's made."

"He's made progress?"

"Oh, yeah. He goes into the backyard now."

"And you think it's because of you?"

"I think he needed a push and I gave him one," she said confidently.

"Lisa, if he finds out you lied, could he get worse than he was before?"

"I don't know. That's why I'm so afraid."

"Okay, hang on a second," Janis said. "So you don't

think Clark will forgive you if you write the paper unless you get Solomon's permission, which could wreck the whole thing?"

"Something like that," Lisa said, staring down blankly at the floor. "And if I write it without his permission, Clark's going to tell him anyway."

"Okay then. I'll say a prayer," Janis added.

Lisa knew she'd need more than a prayer if she was going to keep Clark, Solomon, and the essay. In a perfect world, Solomon would be touched that she'd chosen to find and help him. And Clark would be impressed with her maturity and honesty, so much so that he'd either be honest with her in return or wake up and stop acting like he didn't care about their relationship anymore. But, this wasn't a perfect world—this was the world that Solomon Reed had run away from and the more Lisa thought about it, the less ridiculous that idea sounded to her. After all, wasn't she just trying to run away from the little part of the world that scared her, too?

TWENTY-THREE
SOLOMON REED

Sometimes Solomon had issues with guilt. And he couldn't talk to anyone about it, because he was afraid that would make it worse. He saw it like this: He didn't have any real problems. People starved to death. People got diseases. People's homes burned down, got torn apart by tornadoes, got repossessed. He was a spoiled kid in suburbia who was too high-strung to deal with the real world.

Lisa and Clark came along and made things better, though. Way better. But, that didn't help any with the guilt. In fact, every time they left his house, he'd get a shooting pain deep in his stomach, remembering that this is all he could be for them. And he was scared, too. He was afraid they'd always be waiting for him to change even more than he already had. Being outside had reinvigorated him, sure, but it hadn't made him want to leave the house. It got him closer. Of course it did. But, that was a long time away and he knew it. Now he had everything he needed *and* friends who would come see him, invitation or not. He wasn't so sure this was a step in the direction they all wanted, but he still held out hope that he'd get there eventually, that one day he'd wake up and it wouldn't be enough for him anymore.

Solomon didn't know what it felt like to be in love. He'd seen it a million times, big and sweeping and beautiful in TV and movies. But he'd always wondered what it actually felt like to think about another person that much, to lose himself in someone else. Now he was thinking maybe he knew.

The day after his impromptu skinny-dip with Clark, Solomon called his grandma. It was time, he'd decided. He'd tell her how he felt about Clark and she'd have some pearl of wisdom for him, some Southern saying that would hit him in all the right places and put things into perfect perspective. That, or she'd ask him something inappropriate about gay sex and he'd get too embarrassed to keep talking to her.

"Joan Reed Realty. We'll take you home," she answered.

"Hi, Grandma."

"Michael Phelps? Is that you?"

"Funny. Want to have lunch with your grandson?"

"Well, isn't this a nice surprise. You finally have some time for me? Did your friends drown in the pool?"

"I thought you *wanted* me to have friends."

"I do. You know I'm just picking on you. What do you want, In&Out?"

"You read my mind."

When she got there, Grandma insisted they eat their cheeseburgers outside on the back patio. Solomon was sort of afraid he'd never get to be inside the house with his grandma again.

"What's on your mind?" she asked, taking a bite.

"Nothing."

"You haven't called to invite me for lunch since you were fourteen. So, what's buttering your biscuit?"

"What?"

"What's bothering you. Context clues, Solomon. Context clues."

"Sorry. Umm . . . I think I'm in love."

"You're kidding me," she said, dropping the burger onto her plate. "With Lisa?"

"Clark," he said with a shaky voice.

"Shut up!" she said, nearly shouting. "I can't wait to tell my friends. I'm the first with a gay grandson; they'll be *so* jealous."

"Jealous?"

"Sweetie, come on. I'm hip. You think your grandma hasn't been dancing in West Hollywood before?"

"You have?"

"The gays love me. I think it's my accent."

"It's definitely your accent," he said. "Anyway, so . . . yeah. Clark."

"You can do better," she said bluntly.

"No, Grandma. It's not like that. He's straight."

"I see. This is what's so complicated. You have to date *and* figure out who plays for your team. It must be exhausting."

"I don't want to hurt Lisa's feelings, either."

"Of course not. She's been good to you, Sol."

"I know."

"You sure he's . . . you know . . . not *into* you?" she asked.

"First off, please don't say that. And, yeah, I'm pretty sure."

"Well, I don't know what to tell you. To me, it seems weird for a straight boy to spend all his time with a gay boy. But, just saying that aloud makes me think I'm completely wrong."

"Me too."

"Is he your *best* friend, Sol?" she asked. "Do you guys talk about everything?"

"Pretty much."

"Then you know what you need to do."

"Talk to him?"

"Exactly."

"Thanks, Grandma. I think you're right. I don't want to lose him."

"Just be careful, okay? Don't get your feelings hurt too bad. We are who we are. You know that better than anyone."

Solomon knew the second he told his grandma about being gay that it wasn't a secret anymore. You'll remember that she liked gossip about as much as Solomon liked *Star Trek*, so telling everyone had been his plan from the start. But how would he do it? How do you tell the two people who know everything about you that they actually don't?

He walked into the kitchen and hopped up onto the counter, watching his parents chop vegetables in silence until they acknowledged him.

"What's up, kiddo?" his dad finally asked.

Then this came out:

"Mom, Dad, there's this episode of *The Next Generation* called 'The Drumhead,' and in it, this medical technician named Tarses is accused of sabotaging the ship. The investigator, this super hard-ass, then tells everyone that Tarses lied on his Starfleet Academy entrance application by saying he was one-fourth Vulcan when, in fact, he was one-fourth *Romulan*."

"Fascinating," his dad joked.

"Okay . . . where was I?" he looked all around, like the words were scrolling past him in the air and he was trying to read them. "Right. See, the Romulans. Oh boy, where do I even begin with the Romulans? Things aren't great with them all the time, okay? There's a lot of bad blood. And don't be confused with the original *Star Trek*, because, in that series, the Romulans are *always* bad guys. And in the movie reboots, too. Did you guys see the movie reboots?"

"Yes," his mom said, a confused look on her face. "You're losing us, Sol."

"Anyway, to be a Vulcan is just . . . it's better, right? Because Vulcans are peaceful, and they're all about logic and reason over emotion. But see the Romulans are *all* emotion. Passionate and cunning. It's what *fuels* them. They're always getting pissed and causing a lot of trouble. And, see, the writers were really smart because they created the Romulans to be a counterpoint to the Vulcans, but they made them share the same ancestry. It's so complex. I could go on for days about it, honestly."

"But that would be highly illogical," his dad said in a robotic voice.

"Good one," he said. "But, can you see where lying about being *one* and really being the *other* could get you into some trouble with the Federation?"

"Sure," his mom said. "But what the hell does this have to do with anything, Sol?"

"It has to do with the fact that Tarses lies about who he is and you can just see the guilt ripping him apart. You can see it on his face. And he says it's a mistake that'll be with him for the rest of his life."

"Spill it," his mom said.

"I don't want to make that mistake, okay? I don't want to lie about who I am, even if it doesn't matter. It's who I am. It's part of me."

"What is?" his dad asked.

"I think you already know."

Not many people would consider Solomon Reed lucky. He had debilitating anxiety, a weak stomach, and he was in love with his straight best friend. But in the parent department, he had won the lottery. So, he'd always known that when he finally told them, they'd make him feel like it was no big deal, like it didn't change a thing. They'd say they loved him just like he was, that there was no way they couldn't.

And that's exactly what they did.

TWENTY-FOUR

LISA PRAYTOR

Lisa hadn't been over to see Solomon in two days, and she knew he was probably a little thrown off by it. Or maybe he didn't really need her anymore. Maybe nobody did. But she needed him—at least until she could get out of there for good. Lisa had to be rational about this and stop letting her paranoia about Clark and Solomon jeopardize the entire plan. Whether they were in love or not, she couldn't let Solomon find out about that essay or he may never recover.

She needed to try, one more time, to convince Clark that keeping it a secret was the right thing to do. It wouldn't be easy, though, especially if he was keeping a secret of his own. But, for the time being, she was banking on Clark still being hers and that good ole Lisa Praytor charm to make things right again.

Just before she left her house for Clark's, Lisa decided to check her e-mail. Not surprisingly, it was already signed in to Clark's account. This happened all the time. He didn't have a laptop, and he was always borrowing hers when he came over. Half the time, ever since school had let out, she just let him take it home with him.

She was about to log out when curiosity got the better of her and she started to scroll through his in-box. Most of the messages were from Solomon. She wasn't surprised because her in-box looked nearly the same. Solomon was sort of an insomniac, so sometimes he'd stay up really late and e-mail them links to funny videos or articles about dumb things like that coffee that comes from Asian tree cat feces.

Lisa read over a few of the e-mails before thinking to click on the Sent folder. When she did, the top message was one Clark had written to Solomon the previous night.

Sol-
I was thinking about yesterday and I just wanted
to apologize again if I weirded you out. Let's go
swimming tomorrow. With trunks. Ha-ha.
Clark

Lisa thought about crying, for just a second, but her breakdown at Janis's had destroyed her tear ducts. Instead, she walked downstairs, got in her car, and drove across town to Clark's house. She stood outside the front door for a few minutes before knocking, trying to talk herself out of dealing with this when it still hurt so bad. She just needed him to confess. If he lied to her, it would break her heart. Eventually, instead of knocking, she opened the always unlocked door and walked back to his bedroom.

"You have something you need to tell me?" she said from the doorway.

"What?" He turned back quickly to face her. He was sitting on the floor playing a video game.

"Why were you naked at Solomon's?"

"Are you kidding me? How'd you even know that?"

"I read your e-mail. Just answer the question."

"You read my e-mail?" he asked, getting up off the floor. "Why would you do that?"

"Look, I'm glad I did or you'd try to stretch this out even longer."

"Stretch what out? Can you please tell me what the hell is going on?"

"You want to explain to me what that e-mail meant?"

"I got to Sol's yesterday and the dude was skinny-dipping, so I just dropped my shorts and jumped in. I thought it would be funny."

"It's not."

"It's kind of funny," he said. "He was just out there swimming around naked. I love that guy. He's so weird. I figured it wouldn't bother him. You know I have no shame. I spend most of my time wearing Speedos in front of complete strangers."

"But he's gay. Don't take your clothes off in front of boys who like boys."

"What are you, my grandmother?" he said. "Just because I'm a guy doesn't mean he wants to jump my bones."

"You're right," she said. "But he's obviously in love with you, and I'm not sure the feeling isn't mutual."

"Oh yeah?" he asked, standing up. She wasn't sure she'd ever seen him this angry. "So what you're *really* here to ask is if *I'm* gay?"

"We used to be together all the time, you know. Now I only see you at Sol's. It's like I pick you up, take you to day-care, and then take you home. And most of the time I'm just sitting there watching you guys fawn over each other."

"I can't help we like the same stuff. You're the one who introduced us. And if you think that makes me gay, then maybe you're the last person who should be helping some-one else."

"Why can't you just tell me the truth, Clark?"

"You're really convinced, aren't you? Wow."

"Well, the last time *I* saw you naked, you couldn't wait to get dressed and now I find out you're stripping down at Solomon's like it's no big deal."

"Because it isn't," he said, raising his voice. "Are you seriously *that* insecure?"

Lisa stayed silent for a few seconds, looking up at Clark where he stood. He was so aggravated his eyes were tear-ing over, and he stared down with a look of deep disap-pointment on his face.

"If you're not gay, then what's wrong with us?" she asked quietly.

"I don't know," he said. "All you talk about is getting out of here. And we both know that even if you do get into Woodlawn, the chances of me going somewhere close by are pretty slim."

"I can't afford to go without the essay anyway."

"I'm sure you'll figure something out."

"That's unlikely," she said, standing up. "I feel crazy. I really do. I see the way you look at each other. The way you are together. It's so obvious."

"Look, I can't help whatever feelings Sol has for me, okay? That's not my fault."

"You keep going back," she said. "Don't you think there's a reason you love going over there so much?"

"Yeah," he said. "Because I finally have a friend who isn't completely self-consumed."

"Clark just . . . be who you are and I'll still love you."

"Get out," he said, eerily calm. "Oh my God, get out. I'm done with this."

Clark shut his bedroom door behind her, and she walked slowly down the hallway to the front door. She passed by Drew, shooting basketball in the driveway, but Lisa never said hello or even acknowledged her. She just got in her car and drove off.

If he was telling the truth, then that meant he'd fallen out of love with her for another reason, and she just wasn't ready to accept that. Her suspicions had been right, that was the only logical explanation for Clark's actions. He could deny it all he wanted to, but the second he told her to get out Lisa knew she didn't really know him anymore.

Clark was obviously too afraid to admit the truth. And why wouldn't he be—they lived in a town full of middle-class conservatives and a celebrated high school athlete coming out of the closet would be big news. And being the one gay guy on the water polo team did *not* sound like the kind of attention Clark would ever want or need. So she could see why telling her the truth was so hard for

him and why asking her to leave had been the smartest
thing Clark could've done. Now she could help him, despite the heartache it would cause her.

She drove to Solomon's house and parked in the driveway.
She knew he'd probably be outside where he wouldn't hear
the doorbell, so she hopped the back fence. She immediately saw Solomon floating on a raft in the middle of the
pool. He had on sunglasses, so she wasn't sure if he was
asleep or awake until she stepped closer and he turned
her way.

"Lisa! Thank God. It's too quiet here."

"Hi," she said, slipping off her flip-flops and sitting at
the edge of the pool. She put both feet in and Solomon
paddled his raft over toward her.

"What's up? Where's Clark?"

"Home," she said. "We kind of had a fight."

"Oh, I didn't know you guys did that."

"We don't. Not usually. I don't know. He's been acting
weird lately."

"Weird how?"

"Well, I really only see him if it's over here. And, not
that I don't like hanging with you or whatever, but, you
know, it would be nice to get some time alone."

"No, I get it," he said, a guilty look on his face.

"I think he likes you," she said, biting her lip and getting
it over with.

"What?" He took off his sunglasses.

"I think maybe he likes you how he used to like me."

"I don't think so, Lisa. You just need to talk to him."

"I've known Clark for a long time, and I've never seen him as happy as he is over here. He gets around you and it's like he turns into a little kid again. And you can't tell me you don't feel the same. I know you do."

"Lisa, I . . ."

"It's okay. I'm not mad. Please don't think I'm mad. I just didn't expect him to reciprocate, that's all. I thought we were safe."

"Safe? Wow."

"No, I didn't mean it like that."

"I came out to my parents yesterday. My grandma, too."

"Really? That's so great, Sol."

"Is it? Or is it *dangerous*?"

"Come on."

"Nothing's happened, just so you know. I'd never do that to you."

"I know," she said. "But maybe you should."

"What?"

"I think he's stuck. He doesn't want to break my heart, maybe."

"Oh," he said, sliding off the raft and into the water. He waded over and leaned against the side of the pool by her legs.

"Do you love him?" she asked, looking down.

"That doesn't matter."

"Yes it does. Do you? I think maybe you do."

"I think so, yeah," he said. "Sorry."

"We've never had sex, you know? Not once."

"I didn't. We don't really talk about that kind of stuff."

"Never? It can't be games and TV all the time."

"It sort of is, though. He isn't one for serious conversation. I'm sure you know that."

"I do. But I think he's just scared. Maybe he's waiting for you."

"This is so fucking weird. What is it you want me to do, Lisa?"

She'd never seen him so frustrated and, all at once, she realized how heavy this must've been weighing on him. Maybe he'd loved Clark this whole time. If Janis could find her soul mate at Camp Christ Is Risen, then surely it was possible for the two of them to fall in love playing dorky strategy games and watching shows about space travel.

"Tell him how you feel," she said. She was holding back tears that had somehow found a way to fill her eyes.

"What if you're wrong?"

"I'm never wrong," she said. "Tell me a good reason you two aren't perfect together, and I'll let you off the hook. I can learn to deal with this. I'd rather it be you than anyone else. It'll just be weird at first. Then maybe we'll laugh about it someday. Like, *Hey, remember when Clark and Lisa were together? That was a mistake, wasn't it?*"

"No one's going to say that."

And then she saw that look on his face and was ready to help him count to ten and breathe slowly and get out of the pool. But this time it wasn't a panic attack. He was crying.

"I tried so hard not to love him, Lisa. Please know that," he said quietly.

"I do," she said. "It's not easy."

"See why I am the way I am? You people are too complicated."

"You're outside right now *and* you're in love. You're one of us, dude."

"Shit," he said. "I can't do it."

"You can," she said. "I know you can. And even if I'm wrong, won't you be glad you told him? So it's not torturing you?"

"I guess," he said. "But what if he never talks to me again?"

"He's not like that," she said. "He's Clark. He'll be okay."

"So if he wouldn't tell you, what makes you think he'll tell me?"

"He won't have to," she said. "You'll both just know. It's like that with love."

"Well, the second I step outside, everything starts going to total shit."

"There's no escaping it."

"What?"

"Life."

"Say you're sure," he said. "Please."

She thought about the question for a few seconds. She was sure of many things: that she wanted as far away from Upland as possible, that her mother would always be sad and lonely, and that Solomon would keep getting better, with or without her. These were inevitabilities. Time would prove that. But was this inevitable, too? Were Solomon and Clark meant to be together?

"Yeah," she answered. "I'm sure."

TWENTY-FIVE
SOLOMON REED

By all accounts, Solomon was doing better than ever. He had friends, he was going outside again, and his panic attacks were at a three-year low. Everything was looking up for him, considering how he'd spent the last few years. But now, with the thought of Clark secretly reciprocating his feelings and what that could mean for the three of them, Solomon couldn't help wondering how quiet and safe his life would still be had the two of them never shown up.

He didn't have much time to think about what he'd do, though, because just an hour after Lisa left, he heard someone banging on the front door. It was Clark, covered in sweat and bent over trying to catch his breath.

"Are you okay?" Solomon asked from inside the house.

"I . . . yeah . . . I just . . ." he said through his heavy breathing. "I just ran like four miles, I think."

"From your house?"

"Yeah."

"Impressive."

"Is it a million degrees out or what?"

"Come in," Solomon said, stepping out of the way. "I'll get you some water."

Clark followed him into the kitchen and chugged two whole glasses of water. He leaned back against the counter, his hair dripping with sweat, and looked over at Solomon like he needed to tell him something. For a split second, Solomon got a rush in his chest like maybe it was about to happen—like the world he ran away from had still managed to send someone just for him. All Clark had to do was say it.

"What did she tell you?" he asked instead.

"She said you guys had a fight." Solomon gripped the sides of the counter where he sat and tried not to let Clark see him shake.

"Did she tell you what it was about?"

"Sort of."

"She thinks we're having a torrid affair or something." Clark started to laugh, but stopped himself when he saw his friend's face.

"I think I love you," Solomon said, staring down at the floor.

"Oh. Don't do that, man."

"Why?"

"You know why."

"Oh my God," Solomon said. "She was wrong."

"Sorry," Clark said.

"For what?"

"That . . . this is the way it is, I don't know. Sorry I can't be different."

"This is the weirdest day of my life."

"Mine too," Clark said. "Why doesn't she believe me?"

"I don't know."

"We've ruined your life, haven't we? We just showed up and brought all this bullshit with us."

"You haven't ruined anything."

"It'll be fine, right? Things will go back to normal and we'll laugh this all off."

"We will?"

"Of course we will," Clark said. "Unless I wake up gay one day and then everybody wins."

Clark cringed, obviously afraid it hadn't landed right. But Solomon knew he was just being Clark—the guy who could always find a way to make you feel better than you should be feeling.

"Shut up," Solomon said. "I can't believe she did this."

"What do I do, man?"

"Do you still love her?"

"I think so."

"You *think* so?"

"I've never fallen out of love before, so I think I still do, but maybe I just don't know the difference."

"You'd know," Solomon said. "You just have to look at your life before her and then after her and see which one you like better."

"I don't think it's that easy."

"Shouldn't it be, though?"

Solomon hopped down from the counter and waved for Clark to follow him. They walked out into the backyard and each took a seat by the pool. For a few minutes, neither of them said anything. It seemed like a perfectly normal thing to do by a pool, to sit there soaking up the sun in silence, but it was about to make Solomon lose his mind.

"Why does she hate it here so much?" he asked.

"She's not like us, man."

"What do you mean?"

"Her family. There's always some drama. Her mom . . . she just . . . she's not great. She's nice enough, but everything's got to be about her. You live long enough with somebody like that and getting as far away as possible becomes your best option. I think that's what happened with Lisa's dad, but she never talks about it."

"And you like it here."

"I do. It's home, you know? I've got my family. I've got you now. I don't need to leave."

"Me neither."

"Dude, I hope you don't take this the wrong way or anything, but I'd switch places with you in a second."

Solomon believed him, too. It was the thing they had most in common—all they wanted was a quiet place to be invisible and pretend the world away. And that's exactly what they had before things got weird. Now, no matter what they told themselves or each other, it would always be different. After all, no first love goes away overnight, especially one that's always right in front of you, but just out of your reach.

TWENTY-SIX

LISA PRAYTOR

"**A**re you okay?" Lisa's mother shouted, standing in the driveway, where Lisa had been sitting for ten minutes with her car engine running.

"What?" Lisa yelled, opening the door.

"Oh good. I thought you were dead."

"What're you doing home?"

"We need to talk."

Lisa followed her mother inside and after a few minutes of watching her bang around in the kitchen as she made tea, Lisa couldn't take anymore.

"Mom, it's been a really long, weird day, so if you could just . . ."

"Ron got a job," she interrupted.

"Okay."

"In Arizona."

"Oh."

"And, after talking about it a lot. A *whole* lot, well, we just think it's best to go our separate ways."

"You're getting a divorce?"

"Eventually, yes."

She was surprised her mom wasn't crying. She almost seemed relieved about it, so Lisa wasn't sure if she should console or congratulate her.

"You seem okay."

"I am. It just wasn't meant to be, I guess."

"Sorry," Lisa said. "Are we moving again?"

"No, honey. I'm keeping the house."

"Thank God."

"Are you going to tell me what's wrong? Why you were catatonic out there in the car?"

"I think it's over with Clark."

And *then* her mom cried. Not much, but she was definitely holding back tears as she listened to the whole story. Lisa told her everything, too—every little detail, from the essay to the conversation she'd just had with Solomon. And she told her about Clark and the secret she was so convinced he was keeping, too.

"I don't see it," her mom said. "But what do I know? Everybody's gay these days."

"I guess I thought we'd always be together."

"That's what everyone thinks when they're seventeen. Believe me."

"Weren't you with my dad at seventeen?"

"Yep. And you see how that turned out. I thought I'd be Mrs. Jacob Praytor forever. He wasn't gay, he was just an asshole. Funnier than anyone I've ever met. But a total asshole."

"Clark's the nicest person I know," Lisa said.

"Me too. But if this is the way it is, then what can you do? At least it isn't your fault things didn't work out."

"At least."

"Is Clark going to tell him? About the essay?"

"I don't think so," she said. "But who knows? I never got the chance to ask him not to."

"You really want into that school, don't you?"

"It's the second-best psych program in the country," Lisa said.

"*Your experience with mental illness.* You could just write anything. Seems like a dumb topic to me."

"They're looking for the right story," she defended. "Something ambitious and courageous."

"Lying isn't courageous."

"You should know."

"Watch it," her mom snapped. "Don't start a fight just because it's the easiest thing to do."

"Sorry."

"So, can you fix it?"

"Probably not."

"Lisa," her mom said, looking her right in the eyes. "I've never heard you say you couldn't do something. Not in your entire life."

Even when Lisa was super busy, she and Clark always kept in touch with a quick phone call or a text. Just to check in. They'd even talked while she was at camp, long enough to say hello and discuss Solomon's progress. But now, a day after he kicked her out of his house, Lisa hadn't heard a word out of Clark.

She hadn't heard from Solomon, either, which made her worry even more. Were the two of them together now?

Maybe Solomon had taken her advice, professed his love, and they were already living happily ever after without her. But, didn't she deserve to know? She was the only reason they even knew each other. And you'd think Clark, of all people, would have the decency to break up with his girlfriend before getting his first boyfriend. What the hell was going on?

When she called Clark's house, Drew answered and said he'd spent the night at Solomon's. Now Lisa was almost certain the truth had finally come out. To her knowledge, he'd never stayed the night at Solomon's, not even once. So, why was he suddenly doing it now?

Later that evening, at just about dark, Lisa grabbed her keys and walked out to her car. She didn't know what she'd say or do, but she had to see them. And if it hadn't been such a weird week, and she hadn't spent the afternoon watching Ron pack up his things while her mom cried in the kitchen, Lisa might not have had it in her to drive to Solomon's and climb over the back fence.

But she did. And now she was standing in the backyard, the only light coming from the swimming pool in front of her. And before she could turn around to face the house, she heard the glass door sliding open.

"Lisa?" Solomon asked. He was standing in the doorway in swim trunks.

"Hey," she said. "You alone?"

Right when she asked it, Clark stepped out behind him holding two cans of soda.

"Lisa," he said, frozen in place. "Hi."

"I guess nobody's taking calls today," she said.

"Sorry," Clark said. "My phone died last night and I didn't bring my charger."

"You stayed the night?" she asked. They were all still standing there, Clark and Solomon by the door and Lisa about ten feet in front of them just barely visible in the pool light.

"Stayed too late and didn't want to walk home."

"Do you want to come sit down?" Solomon asked, shooting Clark a look asking for approval.

"Yeah, come on," Clark said. "It's freezing."

They walked over to the pool and Clark draped a towel over his bare shoulders. Then he threw one to Lisa and one to Solomon, who each did the same. He took the seat right between them and they both stared at him, expecting him to speak first.

"You were wrong," he said to Lisa in an almost amused, but still quiet tone.

"I was?"

"Not gay," Solomon added, shaking his head.

"Shit," she said. But it was low and weak, not angry. She sat there for a few seconds not looking up at them. She wasn't one to blush, but she was sure her cheeks were on fire and she hoped the darkness would cover it up so she wouldn't be mortified even more.

"At least you didn't let it get out of hand," Clark said sarcastically.

"So I guess you told him then?" Lisa said to Clark.

"What? No." He shook his head and widened his eyes so she would drop it. But, it was too late.

"Told me what?" Solomon asked.

She wanted so badly to lie, to have just a little more time before being unmasked as a complete monster. But it was over now. It had to be over.

"About the essay," she said, closing her eyes tightly.

"What essay?"

"Shit," Clark said.

"Solomon . . . it seemed like such a good idea, and I didn't know it would be like this. I didn't know *you* would be like this. That you'd be *you*. And now . . ."

"Lisa, what the hell are you talking about?"

"It's an admissions essay," Clark said. "To Woodlawn."

"So what?" he said. "I mean . . . what about it?"

"They give one full paid scholarship a year to the candidate with the best essay," Lisa said.

"I'm really confused. . . ."

"It's supposed to be about her personal experience with mental illness," Clark blurted out.

"It's a psychology program?" Solomon asked.

"Yeah."

"I thought you wanted to be a doctor."

"I never . . ."

"You never said what kind," Solomon interrupted. "So I guess I'm . . ."

"You're her personal experience with mental illness," Clark said.

"You knew?" Solomon asked. Clark just nodded his head with this expression of total defeat on his face.

"You guys need to leave," Solomon said quietly. His voice was deep and sad and nearly unrecognizable.

"Sol, I . . ." Clark began.

"Leave," he said, standing up. He started to pace along the edge of the pool and he let the towel fall from his shoulders and into the water.

"I'll get that," Lisa said.

"Leave it alone!" Solomon shouted. "Get out! Go home! Both of you! Go home!"

Tears were smeared across his face and even in the faint pool light, you could see the panic in his eyes. Lisa stepped toward him, but he jerked back, almost falling into the pool. She begged him to sit down and take deep breaths, and so did Clark, but he was too far gone. The more they tried to help, the more he paced and twitched and yelled for them to leave. It didn't take long for his parents to come outside, and when his dad put an arm around him he shoved him to the ground. Then, just as he went in to try again, Solomon took his right hand, raised it into the air, and then slapped it hard across the side of his own face. And then he did it again, so hard that his mom whimpered a little and ran over to hold his arms back.

Through the house, and out to the front door, they could still hear him yelling. Lisa closed the door behind her and stopped to take a deep breath, like she'd just escaped from a monster in a dream. Even from the driveway, as they got into Lisa's car, they could hear Solomon's parents trying to calm him down. But he wasn't calming down. He was yelling and throwing things. Lisa heard something hit the side of the house. Maybe he'd thrown a chair or one of those little garden gnomes his mom had all around the yard. Then, just as Lisa was about to crank the car, one loud yell from Solomon's dad echoed through the neighborhood. "Damn it, Solomon! Stop!" And everything got really quiet.

As they backed out of the driveway, Lisa eyed the house with tears trickling down her cheeks. She looked over to Clark, who had his face completely covered with his hands. His legs were shaking up and down like he couldn't stop them and a few times on the drive to his house, she thought she heard him crying. Solomon's world had become his, too, and it looked like she'd just destroyed it. It was all over now.

After she dropped a still-silent Clark off at home, her *good-bye* never met with a response, she drove back to Solomon's and parked across the street. She stayed there, watching the dark, quiet house for over an hour. She didn't do it because he needed her. She did it because she was afraid the farther she got from him, the better off he'd become. And despite spending most of her time thinking about leaving, Lisa wasn't ready to go just yet.

TWENTY-SEVEN
SOLOMON REED

He'd been hitting himself like that for years, but it was the first time anyone outside of his family had seen it. Now he would always remember the looks on their faces—right after the first strike.

They'd been so real, Clark and Lisa. It had felt so real that he'd never stopped to question why it was happening—why they'd waste their time on someone like him in the first place.

He lay awake that night, touching the side of his face a few times, remembering what he'd done. It hadn't happened in a long while, maybe more than a year. It hadn't happened that day at school, either. But at home, that same day he'd jumped into the fountain, he'd gotten so anxious, pacing around the living room listening to his parents try to calm him, that he suddenly just lost it completely and slapped his face. He immediately started crying, confused and guilty, looking up at his parents like he had no idea how it had happened. And, really, that's the way it always was with the hitting. It would happen so fast, his body shaking to release the tension built up from all the thoughts swirling through his mind and all the air he was having trouble breathing and all the loud beating of his own heart ringing in his ears. It had to get out and that was the path it chose. Slap. Instant relief.

The next day, Solomon didn't go outside. It was just like every other day before he'd met them—familiar in a way that made him nostalgic and nauseated. Part of him wished he could go back in time and tear Lisa's weird ass friendship letter in half. He thought maybe he could pretend them away, like he did so many other things. Out of sight, out of mind.

He looked up the Woodlawn University School of Psychology's admission guidelines and read all about the Jon T. Vorkheim Scholarship, which was full paid tuition awarded to the candidate with the *highest need of assistance and highest likelihood of bringing a new perspective to the field of Psychology based on his/her personal experience with mental illness.*

"Shit," he said aloud to nothing but an empty house.

A week later, he still hadn't gone outside. And he was still refusing to take calls from Clark or Lisa. He spent most of his time holed up in his bedroom with the door shut and, for the most part, his parents left him alone. They knew Solomon better than anyone and if he needed the time to himself, they weren't about to take it away.

When Clark showed up to get his van, Solomon couldn't talk himself into seeing him. So, Clark said a quick hello to Valerie and followed Jason to the garage, where they got the engine started and had him on his way. Afterward, Solomon's dad knocked lightly on his door before walking in and sitting on the edge of his bed.

"Sort of sucks to see it go," he said.

"What? The van?"

"Yeah. Got used to having a project. Thing barely runs, but at least it runs."

"How is he?"

"Sad, Sol. He looked pretty sad."

"Yeah, well . . ."

"I don't think he meant any harm," his dad interrupted. "Guilty by association, I guess. But he's been a good friend to you."

"But he knew. How do I know if any of it was real?"

"Because you know. C'mon."

"I don't know what I know."

"You ever going outside again?" his dad asked, looking him right in the eyes.

"Why's it matter?"

"I can't answer that," he said, stepping out into the hallway. "But when you can tell me it doesn't, I'll quit asking."

Later that day, Solomon's dad was reading a book in the living room when his son walked through, still wearing the pajamas he'd had on for days, a guilty look on his face.

"It emerges," his dad said. "From the room of eternal stench."

"Okay, that's not fair."

"Have you had a bath this week?"

"Maybe not."

"Where are you going?"

"Outside, I think."

"Look, I'm sorry for . . ."

"Dad," he interrupted. "Don't be."

Solomon looked out at the blue water across the yard and then over at his dad, who pretended not to be watching. Then he turned back to slide the door open, this thing he'd done hundreds of times like it was no big deal. Only, as soon as the outside air touched his face, his heart started beating faster and faster and he suddenly couldn't catch his breath. Everything turned so loud and shaky that suddenly the pool looked farther away, too far to reach. And by the time his dad got over to him, he was sitting on the tile floor with his knees up and his face tucked between them.

When it was over, he looked up at his dad with this hopeless expression on his face. And in that silent moment, just before he walked back to his room and shut the door, he knew they were thinking the same thing—that maybe it would always be this way.

Eventually, Solomon would stop trying to go outside altogether. The panic attacks would subside and they'd all pretend those few months away, not wanting to feel the pangs of nostalgia it gave them to think about the two weird kids who showed up one day and made everything better.

Solomon stayed in his room until his grandma came over for dinner that night. He knew he wouldn't be able to avoid her, so he was dressed and ready when she got there. He tried to plant a smile on his face, but it wasn't working and she could tell. So, when she went to kiss his cheek, she whispered *You're okay* into his ear and patted his back lightly.

He didn't talk much at dinner, which was easy since his grandma was over. He just chewed his food in silence while she rambled on and on about a difficult new home-buyer she'd been dealing with earlier that day. He'd been listening to her describe the ins and outs of the suburban realty world for his entire life, and it was always a lot more darkly humorous and twisted than you'd think. This particular story involved an extramarital affair *and* a pol-tergeist. No joke.

After dinner, Grandma asked if he wanted to get his butt kicked at a game of cards and, although he hesitated at first, he couldn't say no. She dealt a hand of canasta at the dinner table, eating her dessert and sipping coffee. Solomon's parents went to the kitchen to do dishes and as soon as they were out of sight, he knew he was in danger. Grandma didn't mince words, and this was the first time he'd been alone with her since he'd gone back to his old ways.

"Remember, twos and jokers are wild," she said.

"Okay."

Five minutes in and not a word had been spoken be-tween them. She was typically an aggressive game player, but her shift from funny storyteller at dinner to serious, poker-faced card shark was throwing Solomon for a loop. Eventually, at the end of one of his turns, he broke down and said something.

"Listen . . . I'm sure I'll be able to go back out there sooner or later."

She didn't respond at first, but instead set her cards down and took a sip of coffee.

"I tried. I did. Earlier today. Did Dad tell you? I bet he told you."

"Solomon," she interrupted. "I don't care about that."

"Oh," he said. "I thought maybe you were . . ."

"Why haven't you seen your friends?" she asked.

"You know why."

"They were helping, you know? I've never seen you so happy."

"They were *lying*."

"So they're not perfect," she said. "You're better with them than without them."

"She was using me, Grandma," he defended. "She was using your *crazy* grandson to get into college. How does that make you feel?"

"I never said it was right. But do you really think that's all it was? You don't need to spend every day with someone just to write a few paragraphs, Solomon."

"Then she tells me Clark's gay, that she's sure of it, and of course—he *isn't* after all, and now I'm back to where I started and I wish I hadn't met either of them in the first place. That would make this better."

"You must really miss them," she said, stone-faced.

"I do."

"Let me tell you something," she said. "I spent a good part of my life being unhappy. I was stuck in my shitty little hometown for longer than I thought I could take. But I got out. It was life or death. And that decision led to every good thing that ever happened to me. Now, I don't know what you want your life to look like. And I won't pretend to understand what it feels like when you're at your worst. I can't imagine how awful it must be. But, I know what it's like to constantly think about a life you aren't living. That's exactly how I felt when I was sixteen and if there was anything I could have done about it, I would have. I know it's easier said than done. I know that. But, you have to try, Solomon. Just look at me. The older I get, the smaller my world gets. And there's not a damn thing I can do about it, either. Life is short, kiddo. You have to at least *try* to live it before you end up where I am—counting down the days till they decide to put you somewhere you can't escape from. That's what I have to look forward to, you know? Having someone else wipe my ass in some place full of dying people."

"Good lord, Grandma."

"Now look at yourself," she said. "Young and smart. This world could be anything you want it to be. Maybe my time's running out, but at least I'm living. And if that's what this is for you, being here inside where nothing ever happens, where you think you're safe, then stay. Stay right here and you let me know how that works for you. Because I'm guessing it'll never really be enough."

"Maybe not."

"I think you can do it," she said. "And you've got plenty of time before I wither away and die to prove me right."

"You said you've got what, like twenty years left?"

"At least. I quit smoking in the eighties, so maybe twenty-five or thirty. You'll have your father's hairline by then, no doubt."

"Okay. Fine. I promise I'll go outside before you kick it."

"Attaboy," she said, looking down at her cards.

For the rest of the game, he kept picturing her stuck in a nursing home somewhere, sad and lonely and wishing he'd come see her, wishing he *could*. He was afraid of the world, afraid it would find a way to swallow him up. But, maybe everyone was sometimes. Maybe some people can just turn it off when they need to.

After his grandma left, all he could think about was growing old and running out of time, so he used the surprising rush of courage it gave him to walk back to his bedroom, dial Clark's phone number, and wait for an answer.

"Hello."

"Hey," he said, his voice raspy.

"Are you okay, man?"

"I think so. I mean, yeah. I will be."

"I'm so sorry. I don't know what else to say . . ."

"I bet you tried to talk her out of it," he interrupted.

"A few times."

"So why didn't you tell me?"

"I was going to, then you told me how you felt and I . . . I didn't want to make it worse."

"Did you want to meet me or was it part of her plan or whatever?"

"I asked to meet you," he answered. "But she told me it would help, too."

"You want to know how I know you love her?" Solomon asked.

"How?"

"Because you kept her secret. You protected her."

"I was protecting her *and* you," Clark corrected.

"Have you talked to her?"

"No. She texts me every morning, but I haven't answered yet."

"Are you going to?"

"After everything she's done?"

"Yeah."

"Probably. How ridiculous is that?"

"Not at all," Solomon said. "I'd forgive you for the same."

"You know I came and got my van, right?"

"The holodeck's not the same without it."

"How are you feeling?"

"Do you really care or are you asking for Lisa? So she can record it in her notes?"

"I don't know what she was thinking," Clark said. "But I know she wanted to help you. It wasn't just about her, man. If you can believe that."

"I'll work on it," Solomon said. "I better go. Thanks for talking to me."

"Oh. Yeah. Of course. I'm really . . ."

Solomon hung up because he knew if he heard any more, he'd start panicking. And then who knows how long it would be before he was breathing normal again and not pacing around the room or crying.

He knew eventually, when he was able to see or talk to Clark without losing his mind, that things between them would be okay. As far as Lisa was concerned, though, he wasn't so sure when he'd be ready to see her again—or, if he'd ever be. But it made him sad to think of his life without her. She'd be like that one missing game piece that you try to forget about or replace but can never quite shake the memory of. And if he missed her this much after a week, then what would a month or a year feel like without her? Maybe he'd never have to find out. At least that's what a big part of him was hoping.

TWENTY-EIGHT

LISA PRAYTOR

Two weeks of radio silence from Clark and Solomon had driven Lisa to a very lonely, strange place. She'd even stayed up late several nights in a row watching reruns of *Star Trek: The Next Generation* on cable. She liked to think that at least one of them was watching with her, or maybe they were watching together, despite everything she'd put them through. It wasn't such a bad show, she discovered. It had some pretty cheesy parts in just about every episode, but when she was finally able to set that aside, Lisa started to see why Solomon and Clark loved it so much.

She'd fully expected Solomon to shut her out—what she'd done to him was unforgivable and she knew it could be a long time before she saw him again, if ever. But with Clark ignoring her calls and texts, Lisa was starting to worry that she'd lost him for good, too.

So, after thirteen days of restraining herself, Lisa drove over to Clark's and marched up the stairs to the front door. She knocked three times, hoping she wouldn't be left out there like she deserved to be. And when Clark's dad opened the door, she couldn't stop herself from giving him a hug.

"Oh, hi, Lisa," he said, lightly patting her back with one hand. "Get him out of the house, will you? He's driving me crazy."

She walked down the hall to Clark's half-open door and pushed it slowly, waiting for him to see her. The room smelled like him—like his deodorant and that cologne his mom bought him every Christmas. He was sitting on the floor, his back against his bed, and reading a book. When he saw her, and their eyes met, he didn't move. For a second, she thought maybe they'd laugh or something. If they both decided to brush the whole thing off as some big joke, then maybe they'd survive it.

"Sit down?" he asked, moving his legs out of the way.

Lisa took a seat on the floor across from him and, instinctively, started to lift her legs to set them on top of his. But she stopped herself just before he noticed. She'd planned to open with an apology, for it to be the very first thing out of her mouth, but he knew she was sorry. He knew everything about her.

"Have you talked to him?" she asked instead.

"Once."

"Is he okay?"

"I think so. It was brief."

"Clark, look, I . . ."

"Do me a favor, Lisa?"

"Sure."

"Don't apologize."

"Okay," she said, not used to this kind of assertiveness from him.

"Good," he said. "Let's figure us out later."

"What do we do about Sol?"

"It was the scariest thing I've ever seen," he said. "He just lost it."

"I'm such an idiot," she said.

"You were supposed to change your mind."

"I was?"

"Yes!" he raised his voice. "My God."

She'd never heard him talk to her like that before, with so much disappointment and anger in his voice. It actually frightened her a little to see this side of him she didn't know was there.

"I guess I gave you more credit than you deserve," he said. "Now I'm an asshole, too."

"Wow, thanks."

"You're welcome," he snapped.

"I don't know what happened," she said. "I got so caught up. And then Janis said . . ."

"You know she hates me. Why would you listen to her?"

"I don't know," she blurted out, hiding her face in her hands.

"And even if you were right, do you think I'd cheat on you? It's like you forgot who I was or something."

"I thought we were figuring us out later?"

"Maybe there's no hope."

"For us?"

"For anyone," he said. "I'm betting Sol's not any better off than he was a week ago, and I could tell just by his voice that he was barely hanging on."

"Shit," she said quietly. "I *am* an asshole. I'm a total asshole."

"You're not a *total* asshole."

"I accused you of cheating *and* I thought you were gay."

"Only one of those makes you an asshole," he said. "I should've realized you felt left out. Honestly, I just didn't think you cared that much."

"Why wouldn't I care?"

"Because, like I said before, all you think about is leaving."

"In a year."

"Yeah, well, I don't want to spend the next year with someone who's just going to leave and forget about me."

"I want you to come with me," she said. "Have you even looked at any schools yet?"

"No," he said. "I like it here. I don't even know if I want to go to college anywhere."

"Oh. Well, why all the water polo then?"

"Because I *like* it," he said, frustrated. "And I'm not worried about how every little thing I do is going to get me out of here. That's *your* thing, not mine."

She just looked at him for a second, wishing he'd take it back and say he'd been secretly applying to colleges in Maryland or DC. But instead, he looked away from her as soon as their eyes met.

"Did he tell you he loved you?" she asked,

"Sure did."

"And?"

"*And* it was weird, okay? It made me so sad. I bet this kind of shit happens all the time."

"Probably," she said. "You're so . . . I don't know, *happy* around him. Like, not bored and complainy like you are around your other friends."

"Thanks," he said. "Doesn't make me gay."

"Of course it doesn't."

"Look, I get it. It's not crazy. It's just frustrating. You *know* me. I didn't suddenly start keeping secrets overnight. He's my friend. He's *our* friend. I was just being his friend back."

"I think you're the only reason he ever went outside," she said. "Like if he got better, then maybe you two could . . ."

"How could you *possibly* know that?" he interrupted. "They were digging a damn hole in the backyard before we ever showed up. I didn't do anything to help him."

"Yeah, well, that makes two of us."

A quiet fell over the room after she'd said it—that kind where you're sure the other person is going to say something you don't want to hear.

"We can't just show up over there, can we? And hope he doesn't freak out?" Clark asked.

"No," she said. "At least I can't."

"I'm not going without you."

"I'm so confused. Are we still together?"

"I don't know," he said. "You're the one who wants to be a shrink. You telling me all this doesn't seem a little like self-sabotage?"

"You've spent too much time around me."

"I listen. Even when you think I'm not."

"I love you, you know?"

"Lisa," he said, closing his eyes for a second and taking

a deep breath. She'd never seen him so frustrated. "Two weeks ago you were so convinced I was gay that you told the *only* person in the world you shouldn't have. I'm not sure this is a healthy relationship anymore."

"It was, though," she defended.

"You remember when we first met?"

"Of course. In biology."

"Physics," he corrected. "I know, because I switched my schedule to be in there with you."

"Huh?"

"Only good thing Janis Plutko ever did."

"I had no idea."

"You guys were always together so I finally worked up the nerve to ask her for your number in homeroom. She gave me your schedule instead."

"Oh."

"I sort of fell in love with you during your speech freshman year."

"That was my third best speech to date," she said.

"You talked about *social change* and I thought that was so funny. You were running *unopposed* for a *freshman* senator spot on the student council," he said. "And you took it so seriously."

"Maybe that should've been your warning."

"Maybe," he said. "But it was good, yeah?"

Lisa knew a lot of things about Clark that no one else knew. She knew he called his grandfather every Sunday, like clockwork. And that he'd never had a sip of alcohol, despite, or maybe *because of* having three older brothers. And she knew that as frustrated as he got with his mom, he never talked back to her or came home even a minute after curfew. Clark Robbins was honest and true, like some weird reincarnation of Abraham Lincoln. And without a little help, he'd let this breakup drag on forever just to spare her feelings.

"It was great," she said. "Look, I realize my track record as a friend hasn't been so hot lately, but I think Solomon needs us. Both."

"Since when does he hit himself?"

"Maybe always," she said. "I'd know that if I actually tried to help him like I set out to do."

"That's not your job."

"No, it's not," she agreed. "So . . . umm . . ."

"I don't want to decide right now," he said. "About breaking up."

"Okay."

"You want to see what I've been working on instead?"

"Sure. Just don't make me go back home yet."

She followed Clark out to the apartment parking lot and couldn't believe it when they rounded a corner to see his old green van sitting right there as ugly as ever.

"You got your van back."

"I only saw his mom and dad when I went to get it, though. They said he wasn't feeling well. Then he called me later that night and hung up before I could even apologize."

"He's probably just embarrassed," Lisa said.

"Of course he is. I broke his fucking heart."

"I don't think I've ever heard you say *fuck* before."

"I curse when I'm sad."

"I don't think I've ever seen you sad, either."

"It's all I can think about," he said, leaning against the

van. "Solomon stuck in that house forever with no one to talk to. *We* did that to him. We proved him right. And now we need to figure out how to fix it or I'll never sleep again."

"Clark, what Sol has is a very complicated disorder that is unpredictable by its very nature."

"You're not a doctor yet, Lisa. And we've all got Wikipedia."

"Fair enough," she said. "But nothing we can do is going to cure him. That's what I'm saying. He needs years of therapy. Maybe decades. Staying inside is one thing, beating the shit out of yourself is another."

"Would you still have done it? If you knew how bad he was?"

"Probably," she said. "But clearly my decision-making skills are questionable."

"At least you're honest," he said. "You ready to see?"

Clark walked around to the back of the van and opened the heavy double doors. The entire cab had been painted solid black—the floor, the ceiling, and both walls. As she looked inside, Clark just stood there with a proud expression on his face.

"I can't believe this," she said.

"We totally gutted it. Took both rows of seats out. All the foam inside them was rotting, which is maybe why it smelled like death in there."

"God, I'm just glad it wasn't an animal or something."

"You and me both. Then we took up that gross carpet and ripped out the ceiling fabric."

"I sure will miss that dick drawing your brother left with the Sharpie," Lisa said.

"Yeah . . . Sol's dad thought that was pretty funny. He asked me if I wanted to keep it. Anyway, we also replaced the battery *and* all the belts. It's running a little better than before, but I think it still needs a lot of work."

"So, what's with the black paint?"

"I did that yesterday," he said, showing her his spray-paint-stained hands. "I could've died from the fumes, but I had an idea and just decided to go for it. I need your help on the last part, though."

About an hour later, Lisa was staring into the back of the van, shaking her head. And Clark did the same thing, standing right beside her. She thought, just for a second, that maybe he'd reach over and squeeze her hand like he used to—this little thing that would silently take them back to what they were.

"I'm not sure this'll ever work," she said, still staring.

"Maybe it doesn't have to," he said. "Gestures, you know."

Lisa stayed for a while after that, eating takeout with Clark and watching some home renovation show that his sister put on. It was like old times, really, except for the wary looks she kept getting from Drew. Lisa knew she was pretty protective of her older brother, but this seemed more personal, like maybe Drew was upset that Lisa hadn't been coming around as often as she used to. So, when Clark left the room to take a phone call, Lisa didn't wait too long before quietly getting up to follow him.

"You there, buddy?" Clark said into the phone when she walked into his bedroom.

"What happened?" she whispered.

"I heard his dad's voice and then he hung up."

Clark took the phone away from his ear, looked at the screen, and then looked up at Lisa.

"Do you think everything's okay?" she asked.

Then the phone rang and they both saw Solomon's name on the screen. But as soon as he put it to his ear, Clark had to hold it away because Solomon was speaking so loudly on the other end.

"I need you to come over. Can you come over? I need you to come over *right* now," Solomon said frantically.

"Lisa's with me, okay?"

"Whatever. Just come over, please!" he said before hanging up.

"We'll take the van," Clark said, rushing out and down the hallway.

"It barely runs."

"It *runs*," he said, turning back to face her.

When they got there, all the lights were on and they could see Solomon standing in the front window. Once out of the car, Lisa hurried to the door and without even thinking about it, swung it right open to face him. He was ghost white, but she couldn't have ignored the red hand marks on the right side of his face if she tried. Not knowing what else to do, she stood there waiting for him to say something, to explain what was going on. But he wouldn't talk, not even when Clark walked up behind her and asked if he was okay. Instead, he took a couple of steps forward and collapsed into Lisa's arms, burying his face in her shoulder.

TWENTY-NINE
SOLOMON REED

"Sol?" Lisa said to him.

He let her go and stood up, trying to calm down and gather his thoughts so he'd actually make sense. Clark took charge and put his arm around Solomon's shoulders, leading him over to the couch to sit down.

"My grandma," he said finally, his voice cracking.

"Oh my God," Lisa said. "Is she okay?"

"I don't know," he managed, closing his eyes tightly. "My dad ran in, said she was in a car wreck, and then ran back out. Then my mom called and said she was at Mountain View Medical."

"What do we need to do?" Clark asked.

"I promised her," Solomon said frantically. "I promised her I'd leave the house before she died."

"Sol, you don't . . ." Lisa began.

"I have to go," he said, standing up. "I have to go, right? What if she's dying? What if this is my only chance?"

He paced around the room, looking at both of them, his panic still too strong to let him deal with the other feelings that seeing them had brought on. But they were there. He knew that much, and they didn't have to be.

"I can't do it," Solomon said. "I promised her and I can't do it. There's no way. I haven't even been in the backyard since you guys left."

"Holy shit," Clark said suddenly, looking toward Lisa. "Are you thinking what I'm thinking?"

"Probably not."

"The *van*," he said, his eyes growing bigger.

"The van?" Solomon asked.

"Oh my *God*, the van," Lisa said.

"WHAT ABOUT THE VAN?" Solomon shouted, flinging his arms into the air.

"WE PUT A HOLODECK IN IT!" Lisa yelled back, scaring the shit out of both of them.

"You did?" Solomon asked.

"Yeah," Clark said. "Like, today. I was going to surprise you."

"Will it work?" Solomon asked, turning toward Lisa.

"I don't know," she said.

"Aren't you going to be a shrink or something?" Solomon asked. "Say it'll work."

"It'll work."

Solomon and Lisa waited in the laundry room while Clark backed the van into the garage. A few seconds later, the clunky metal back doors opened and, from where they were standing, it was suddenly hard to tell where the interior of the van ended and the garage began. They'd painted it solid black and used yellow tape to block it off into big squares. There was even a black curtain or something separating the front of the van from the back so when Solomon looked in, all he could see was the same pattern that was surrounding him in the garage.

"I think it looks pretty good," Clark said.

"You did all this for me?"

"Or maybe I just wanted one of my own," Clark said with grin.

"You helped him?" he asked Lisa.

"Yeah. How's it look?"

"Perfect," he said.

He climbed inside, ducking his head down until he was in the center and then taking a seat. He looked all around and then over to where they stood, watching him from just outside.

"How're you feeling?" Clark asked him.

"My heart's racing," he said. "And it smells like paint back here."

"Sorry."

"We need to hurry up," Solomon said. "I can do this, right?"

"Want me to ride with you?" Lisa asked.

He nodded his head and patted the cold, black floor beside him. He could forget who she was today. He could forget what she'd done just long enough to get through this. It was something he had to do. He needed her. He was better the second she showed up at his front door and if there was anyone who could help him do this, it was her.

So she climbed in and they sat side by side, facing the back doors. When Clark closed them, all they could see were yellow boxes filled with solid black nothingness. Lisa let one hand rest in between them and as soon as Clark turned the ignition, Solomon's hand fell down onto hers.

"It's okay," she said calmly. "We're going to just breathe and pretend we're back home."

"And what about when we get there?"

"You guys ready?" Clark shouted from the front seat.

"One second," Lisa answered. "Look, maybe adrenaline will just kick in and you'll be fine. You've heard those stories, right? About the women who lift cars off their kids and stuff? Maybe it'll be like that."

"It won't be," he said.

"Well, let's just get there and see," she said. "We're ready!"

At first, when he felt the van kick into gear, Solomon closed his eyes. It'd been so long since he'd been in a vehicle, feeling it move under and around him. The driveway was slanted, so he could tell when Clark had pulled out and onto the street. That's when he opened his eyes and gripped Lisa's hand a little tighter, staring ahead at the familiar pattern, but knowing full well where he was—out in the world like the rest of them.

"Oh no," he said over the sound of his own heavy breathing. "What am I doing? What am I doing?"

"Let's count to ten, Sol," Lisa said.

"No!" he shouted. "Sorry, I mean . . . I can't . . . maybe we should turn around."

"Clark, slow down." Lisa scooted over in front of Solomon to look him straight in the face, her nose inches from his, the whites of her eyes nearly glowing in the darkness. "Listen to me," she whispered. "You can do this. You already *are* doing this. Take my other hand."

He took her hand and now they were sitting there, on the hard floor of the loud, clunky van, holding hands like they were about to have a séance or something and with every bump, Solomon felt his body tense up. This was no séance. It was torture. And it was getting harder for him to breathe, like he'd been leashed to his house and the collar was choking him the farther away he got.

"Sol," Lisa said calmly. "We're here. I'm here. You're here. We're here and we're moving. Nothing bad will happen. Clark's a good driver. Aren't you, Clark?"

"A great driver!" he shouted back.

"And we're going to get you to your grandma, okay? But you have to do me a favor."

"What?" he said between loud breaths.

"You have to count with me. Let's go. One . . ."

He mumbled the numbers through his frantic breathing, but without her having to say so, he started taking slower, deeper inhalations. "Good," she said. "Where are we?"

"We're in Clark's van."

"No. We're in the garage." She moved back beside him, letting go of one hand but keeping a firm grasp on the other. "And in here, we can relax."

"Lisa . . . I . . ."

"In here, we can be wherever we want to be. You want to be at home? Make it so."

"I want to be in the backyard," he said, his voice shaky with a sense of impending doom hanging all around it.

"It's a great backyard . . ."

"Swimming," he interrupted. Then he closed his eyes again. "Underwater. You know when you try to keep yourself at the very bottom and look all around. How it's so quiet?"

"Yeah," she said. "I love that."

"Me too. I love how you can only move so fast in water, you know? As long as it's all around you, you're kind of safe from everything."

"Air can be like that," she said. "It's particles. It's more like water than it is like nothing."

His eyes opened and he turned to her. He smiled, but just for a second, and then he thought about the air between them—how he could see right through it and how she was seeing him, too. He could certainly smell it, wondering for a brief second if maybe the paint fumes were really what was keeping him sedated, and not Lisa's distraction therapy.

"How much longer?" he asked.

"Ten minutes, tops."

Lisa took her phone out and found Valerie Reed's number. As she waited for an answer, she kept a tight grip of Solomon's hand and made sure he was still breathing right.

"Straight to voice mail," she said, still holding the phone up to her ear.

"Shit shit shit," Solomon said, rocking back and forth.

"Dr. Reed, this is Lisa. We have your son. We're on our way. Please call back if you can."

"Great," Clark said. "Now we're kidnappers."

"She's gonna die without ever knowing," Solomon said.

Solomon tried to focus on breathing. And counting, which he'd never stopped doing in his head that whole time. He would take a slow breath, exhale when he got to five, and then do it again. Over and over until he felt the van stop.

"We're here!" Clark said.

"Don't open the doors," Solomon whispered, trying to stay calm.

"They're sealed till you say so, pal," Clark said.

"What do you want to do, Sol?" Lisa asked.

"Can you go find them? See if she's okay? *Joan Reed.*"

"Joan. Got it," she said, standing up. "Don't turn around."

She opened the curtain and squeezed by Clark as he made his way to the back. He sat down beside Solomon, who stared straight ahead and pretended not to be there. So, Clark just looked all around and then back at his friend before letting out a loud sigh and turning his way.

"What?" Solomon asked.

"You're out here, man. Weird, right?"

"You're supposed to be distracting me."

"Oh . . . umm . . ."

"Are you and Lisa okay?"

"To be determined," Clark said.

"Thanks," Solomon said. "For this."

"Wesley Crusher, right? Always saves the day."

"I can't get out of the van, Clark."

"I know, Sol. But you made it pretty damn far."

Then Clark's phone rang and right when he answered, Solomon grabbed it from him.

"Mom? Is she okay? What's going on?"

"She's in surgery. She's pretty beat up and she's got a few broken bones, but she's going to be fine. Where *are* you?"

"Outside," he said, choking back tears. "In the parking lot."

"By the ER," Clark whispered.

"By the ER. Mom? Is Dad okay?"

"We're both fine. Lisa just ran up. I can't *believe* this."

"Me neither," he said. "You'll tell her I was here?"

"As soon as she's awake. First I'm coming to you. Don't move."

They sat there alone in the dark for a while and after a few minutes, despite still counting in his head and trying to focus on his breathing, Solomon looked all around, smiled a little, and then turned to his friend.

"We're okay, Clark," he said, giving him the best smile he could manage. "We're good."

Suddenly, they heard the front door of the van creak open and then, as soon as he turned around, Solomon saw his mom climbing her way toward him. She asked Clark to give them a minute and once they were alone, she scooted a little closer and looked Solomon right in the eyes.

"Your grandma's tough," she said. "A month from now, she'll be bragging about her new car *and* her new hip."

He smiled for his mom, but he still couldn't relax enough to show much emotion. He traced the yellow squares behind her with his eyes until she moved even closer, blocking his view entirely. She didn't break down crying or tell him she was proud of him or promise him that everything was going to be okay. She just looked right at him the only

way she ever had, like he was the only other person in the
world. And then she patted him on one leg and said, "Let's
get you home."

When Lisa was back, she sat in front of him and went
to hold his hand like before. But he quickly drew it away
and instead leaned forward and wrapped his arms around
her shoulders. It was quiet and brief, but that was all it
needed to be. Then he let go, grabbed her hand, and looked
her right in the eyes as the engine started and shook the
van around them.

Back at the house, they waited until the garage door
was completely shut before letting Solomon out. Then Lisa
and Clark followed behind him without saying a word. He
walked straight through the laundry room to the living
room, opened the sliding glass door, and walked out into
the backyard. And by the time Lisa had turned on the
outdoor lights, he'd already jumped into the pool with all
his clothes on.

A few seconds later, he shot up from under the water
in a big, loud splash. "Did that just happen?" he yelled,
wiping water out of his eyes.

"That just happened," Clark said.

Maybe it was the happiest moment of Solomon's life,
but he couldn't be sure. And if he hadn't been looking for
it, he may have missed it, but just before Lisa and Clark
threw their phones into the grass and cannonballed into
the water beside him, he saw them quickly hold hands,
giving one little squeeze before letting go. He'd left the
house. He'd survived it. But damn it felt good to be home,

to be in the water, to be with them. He didn't need to go anywhere else. It was safe here. It was predictable. It was just a tiny little square on the side of the world. He never needed to leave it again.

But that didn't mean he never did.

THIRTY

LISA PRAYTOR

MY PERSONAL EXPERIENCE
WITH MENTAL ILLNESS

My name is Lisa Anne Praytor and I am a senior at Upland High School in Upland, California. One morning, when I was in middle school, a boy I didn't know stripped off his clothes and jumped into the fountain in front of my school. And then he disappeared. For three years, I didn't hear anything else about him. Not a word. But then, one day last spring, I found him. His name is Solomon Reed, and he is my personal experience with mental illness.

But, he shouldn't be. I had no right to do what I did, but he said it was okay. He said I could write this. Not because finding him was the right thing to do, and maybe not because it helped him, but because even though he hadn't been part of the world in three years, Solomon Reed had created one of his own—one that saved his life. And I think he wants you to know that.

The first time I went to his house, I wanted to cure him. Find him, fix him, and get my scholarship. That was the plan. But he wasn't a patient and I wasn't a counselor, so we became friends instead. Then, before I knew it, he was getting better, and it wasn't because of my natural talent for performing cognitive behavioral therapy on sixteen-year-old agoraphobes with panic disorder, either. It was because now he had a reason to get better. So, I thought I should add another reason: my kind and handsome boyfriend, Clark. What better way to tempt a homosexual recluse out of the house, right?

I'm not really sure why I ever thought I was qualified to fuck around with someone's life like I did. I could blame it on age, but that's too easy. Ambition, maybe? After all, this was about getting into your program (and, hopefully, about being able to pay for it). But, I can't just blame you, can I?

I blame all of us.

I'll never forget that day at the fountain. The other kids laughed and whispered, even when the principal had gotten him out of the water and wrapped a jacket around him. They just kept laughing and pointing as he walked by, dripping wet and never looking up from the ground. Most everyone I knew heard some ridiculous gossip about him by the end of that day. But then, within weeks, it was like he'd never existed. And that's when I got the saddest. They never brought him up again. Like we belonged there and he belonged somewhere else. It's not too hard to disappear when no one's looking for you.

That's what we do sometimes. We let people disappear.

We want them to. If everyone just stays quiet and out of the way, then the rest of us can pretend everything's fine. But everything is not fine. Not as long as people like Solomon have to hide. We have to learn to share the world with them.

And I know I'm not one to speak. Ethically, professionally, and morally, I did all the wrong things. I've been a shitty friend and a shitty girlfriend. And I did it all so my future would look different from my past. I wanted to be part of your program so I could help people. And, in the process, I hurt the two people closest to me.

But, they're still here. And Solomon still opens the door every time I come over. We still swim. We still watch movies. We still play games. He isn't the crazy fountain kid. Crazy people don't know they're crazy. And because he knows what makes him lose control, he can learn how to make his world bigger without being buried by it.

I don't suspect I'll be admitted into your program, and I surely won't be awarded the Jon T. Vorkheim Scholarship. But, I'd like to thank you anyway. Without your essay, Solomon would've stayed invisible. And I'd probably still think that getting into your school was the only way to be happy. It's not. As smart as I am, it took a boy stuck in his house to teach me that sometimes it doesn't matter where you are at all. It only matters who's with you.

It's like on *Star Trek: The Next Generation*, really. We're just floating in space trying to figure out what it means to be human. And clearly I need more time to float. When I'm ready to take a step, though, Sol will be there to help me. And so will Clark. The world is big and scary and unforgiving. But we can survive out here. Solomon Reed did. I held his hands and we counted to ten and it was beautiful. He was an astronaut without a suit, but he was still breathing.

THE END

ACKNOWLEDGMENTS

I owe a completely logical amount of gratitude to the many people who had to deal with me as I wrote this book.

Chief among those is Namrata Tripathi, my editor, who always asks why and never lets me get away with not having an answer. Ever. Nami's ability to crack open my skull and extract cohesive narratives is astounding and I'm very lucky to work with her.

Then there's Stephen Barr, my agent, whose insightfulness and kindness can only be measured in tacos. Stephen is the real deal—an agent who always answers phone calls and never minces words. Again, I'm a lucky guy.

I'd also like to say a huge THANKS to everyone at Dial Books and Penguin Random House for welcoming me with such open arms.

And it's very true that I'd be nowhere without libraries, so I want to say a special thanks to all those librarians out there who spend their days putting books in kids' hands. And to all those booksellers who take the special time to match the right book to the right reader.

And finally, a huge thanks to my family and friends. I'm lucky enough to say that there are too many of you to name here, but you know who you are and what you mean to me. I have a very cool job, but it requires lots of inspiration and real-life material. You all give me that. I can't thank you enough.